"You're more attracted to me than you are to Max." He said the words flatly, yet there was a wealth of challenge in them, and he looked at her as if daring her to deny them.

She opened her mouth, then shut it again. She arched her eyebrows at him provocatively. "You think so?"

"You know you are," he insisted. "There's been a spark between us since day one."

This time she opened her mouth and didn't shut it, still trying to formulate the words. She gave a careless, dis⬚⬚⬚⬚⬚⬚ ⬚⬚⬚⬚⬚ "I⬚ ⬚⬚⬚⬚ dreams, Savas."

But Sebastian didn't ⬚⬚⬚⬚ He closed the spac⬚ ⬚⬚⬚⬚ she had to tip her he⬚⬚⬚ ⬚⬚ mouth was bare inches away. She could see the whiskered roughness of his jaw, could feel the heat of his breath.

She swallowed. She blinked. She waited.

And the next thing she knew Sebastian's lips came down on hers.

Award-winning author **Anne McAllister** was once given a blueprint for happiness that included a nice, literate husband, a ramshackle Victorian house, a horde of mischievous children, a bunch of big, friendly dogs, and a life spent writing stories about tall, dark and handsome heroes. 'Where do I sign up?' she asked, and promptly did. Lots of years later, she's happy to report the blueprint was a success. She's always happy to share the latest news with readers at her website, www.annemcallister.com, and welcomes their letters there, or at PO Box 3904, Bozeman, Montana 59772, USA (SASE appreciated).

SAVAS' DEFIANT MISTRESS

BY
ANNE McALLISTER

MILLS & BOON
Pure reading pleasure™

All the characters in this book have no existence outside the imagination of the author, and have no relation whatsoever to anyone bearing the same name or names. They are not even distantly inspired by any individual known or unknown to the author, and all the incidents are pure invention.

First published in Great Britain 2009
Harlequin Mills & Boon Limited,
Eton House, 18-24 Paradise Road, Richmond, Surrey TW9 1SR

© Barbara Schenck 2009

ISBN: 978 0 263 87203 3

Set in Times Roman 10 on 12 pt
01-0509-54528

Printed and bound in Spain
by Litografia Rosés, S.A., Barcelona

SAVAS' DEFIANT MISTRESS

CHAPTER ONE

"I WAS thinking little square boxes with silver and rose jelly beans in them." Vangie was saying breathlessly into the phone.

Sebastian, who wasn't listening, had his attention on the computer screen in front of him. His sister had been rabbiting on in his ear for nearly twenty minutes. But truthfully, she hadn't said anything important in the last three weeks.

"You know what I mean, Seb? *Seb?*" Her voice rose impatiently when he didn't reply. "Are you there?"

God help him, yes, he was.

Sebastian Savas managed a perfunctory grunt, but his gaze stayed riveted on the specs for the Blake-Carmody project, and his mind was there, too. He glanced at his watch. He had a meeting with Max Grosvenor in less than ten minutes, and he wanted everything fresh in his mind.

He'd worked his tail off putting together ideas for this project, aware that it would be a terrific coup for Grosvenor Design to get the go-ahead.

And it would be an even bigger coup for him personally to be asked to head up the team. He'd done a lot of the work. Using Max's ideas and his own, Seb had spent the past two months putting together the structural plans and the public space layout for the Blake-Carmody high-rise office and condo building. And last week, while Seb had been in Reno working on another major project, Max had presented it to the owners.

Still he'd had a big hand in it, and if they'd won the project, it made sense that that was what today's meeting was about— Max asking him to run the show.

Seb smiled every time he thought about it.

"Well, I wondered," Vangie was saying, undeterred. "You're very quiet today. So…what do you think, Seb? Rose? Or silver? For the boxes, I mean. Or—" she paused "—maybe boxes are too fussy. Maybe we shouldn't even have jelly beans. They're sort of childish. Maybe we should have mints. What do you think of mints? *Seb?*"

Sebastian jerked his attention back at the impatient sound of his name in his ear. Sighing, he thrust a hand through his hair. "I don't know, Vangie," he said with just the slightest hint of impatience himself.

What's more, he didn't care.

This was Vangie's wedding, not his. She was the one tying the knot. And since he never intended to, he didn't even need to learn from the experience.

"Why not have both?" he said because he had to say something.

"Could we?" She sounded as if he'd suggested having the Seattle symphony play the music for the reception.

"Have what you want, Vange," he said. "It's your wedding."

It was, to Seb's mind, fast becoming The Wedding That Ate Seattle. But what the heck, if it made his sister happy—for the moment at least—who was he to argue with her?

"I know it's my wedding. But you're paying for it," Vangie said conscientiously.

"No problem."

Where family was concerned, Seb was the one they all turned to, the one who offered advice, a shoulder to lean on and a checkbook that paid the bills. It had been that way ever since he'd got his first architectural job.

"I suppose I could ask Daddy…"

Seb stifled a snort. Philip Savas begat children. He didn't raise them. And while the old man had plenty of money—the family's considerable hotel fortune residing in his pockets—he didn't part with it easily unless it was something he wanted. Like another wife.

"Don't go there, Vange," Sebastian advised his sister. "You know there's no point."

"I suppose not," she said glumly with the voice of experience. "I just wish…it would be so perfect if he'd remember to come and walk me down the aisle."

"Yeah." Good luck, Seb thought grimly. How many times did Vangie have to be disappointed before she learned?

Seb could pay the bills and offer support and see that his siblings had everything they needed, but he couldn't guarantee their father would ever act like one. In all of Sebastian's thirty-three years, Philip Savas never had.

"Has he called you?" Vangie asked hopefully.

"No."

Unless Philip wanted to foist a problem off on his responsible eldest son, he couldn't be bothered to make contact. And Seb was done trying to make overtures to him. Now he glanced at his watch again. "Listen, Vange, I've gotta run. I have a meeting—"

"Of course. I'm sorry. I shouldn't bother you. I'm sorry to bother you all the time, Seb. It's just you're the only one here and…" Her voice trailed off.

"Yes, well, you should have got married in New York. You'd have had all the help you could use then." When Seb had come out to Seattle after university, it had been expressly to put a continent between himself and his multitude of ex-stepmothers and half siblings. He didn't mind supporting them, but he didn't want them interfering in his life. Or his work. Which was the same thing.

His bad luck, he supposed, that when Vangie graduated from Princeton and got engaged, her fiancé, Garrett's, family was from Seattle, and they decided to move here.

"It will be wonderful. I can see you all the time. Like a real family!" Vangie had said at the time. She'd been over the moon at the prospect. "Isn't that great?"

Seb, who had given up any notion of "real family" by the time he'd reached puberty, hadn't seen anything to rejoice in. But he'd managed to cross his fingers and give her a hug. "Terrific."

In fact, it hadn't been as bad as he'd feared.

Vangie and Garrett both worked for a law firm in Bellevue. They spent time with each other and with their own set of friends and he rarely saw them.

He pleaded work whenever they did invite him to one of their parties. It wasn't an excuse; it was the truth.

Vangie said he worked far too hard, and Garrett thought his almost-brother-in-law was boring because he did nothing except design buildings.

That was fine with Seb. They had their lives and he had his.

But as the date for the wedding approached, things had changed. Wedding plans made months ago now required constant comment and consultation.

Vangie had begun calling him daily. Then twice a day. Recently it had increased to four and five times a day.

Sebastian wanted to say, "Get a grip. You're a big girl. You can make decisions on your own."

But he didn't. He knew Vangie. Loved her. And he understood all too well that her wedding plans were symbolic of her biggest fantasy.

She'd always dreamed of being part of a "real" family, of having that built-in support. It was what "normal" families did, she told him.

And Vangie, more than any of them, had always desperately wanted them to be "normal."

Seb was frankly surprised she even knew what "normal" was.

"Of course I know what a normal family is," she'd told him sharply when he'd said so. "And so do you."

He'd snorted at that. But she'd just come back with, "You have to try, Seb. And trust that it can happen."

There was no reply to that. If Vangie wanted to live in a Disney movie, he couldn't stop her. But whenever she called, he let her talk. At least, he did when he didn't have to get to a meeting sooner rather than later.

But Max had left a message on his mobile phone last night while Seb had been flying back from Reno to say they needed to talk this afternoon.

Which meant, Seb thought with a quickening excitement that owed nothing to jelly beans or mints or the color rose, that they'd won the Blake-Carmody bid.

He and Max had spent both many long hours working up a design for the forty-eight-story downtown building that would be a "complete village" with shops, office and living space. And even though Max had been the one who'd taken the main port-folio to meet with Steve Carmody and Roger Blake, Seb knew it was unspoken that he was being groomed for the head architect's position. So he had kept on improving, revising, detailing the general plans.

"I just don't know," Vangie said now. "There are so many things to think about. The napkins, for instance—"

"Yeah, well, we can talk about it later," Seb said with all the diplomacy he could muster. "I really have to go, Vange. If I hear from Dad, I'll let you know," he added. "But he's more likely to ring you than me."

They both knew he wasn't likely to ring either of them. When last heard from, Philip was about to marry his latest personal assistant. She'd be the fourth who'd had her eye on his wealth. At least his old man knew how to do a decent pre-nup at this point.

"I hope so," Vangie said fervently. "Or maybe he's been in touch with one of the girls."

"What girls?" Philip was taking them on in pairs now?

Would it be harems next? Seb wondered, as he shut his portfolio and stood up.

"The girls," Vangie repeated impatiently, as if he should know which ones. "*Our* sisters," she clarified when he still didn't respond. "Our *family*. They'll be here this afternoon," she added, and all at once her voice sounded bright.

"Here? Why? The wedding's not till next month, isn't it?" God knew he was busy, but Seb didn't think he'd lost the whole month of May.

"They're coming to help." Seb could hear the smile of satisfaction in Vangie's voice. "It's what families do."

"For a month? All of them?" He could even remember how the hell many there were. But it didn't sound like anything to rejoice about.

"Just the triplets. And Jenna."

All the ones over eighteen, then. Dear God. How was Vangie going to put up with them all for a month? That ought to make her think twice about how much she wanted all of them to be a "normal" family.

"Well, good luck to you. So you want me to arrange for them to be picked up at the airport?"

"No. Don't worry. They're coming from all over and at different times, so I told them they should just take taxis."

"Did you? Good for you." Seb smiled and flexed his shoulders, glad Vangie was showing a bit of spunk, and grateful that she hadn't stuck him with all the logistics of shifting their sisters around as well as having to listen to the jelly bean monologues. He picked up his portfolio. "Where are they staying?"

He supposed he ought to know that. He might even drop by and take them to dinner on Sunday—in the interests of "normal" family relations.

"With you, of course."

The portfolio slammed down on his desk. "*What!*"

"Well, where else would they stay?" Vangie said reasonably.

"All those rooms just sitting there! You must have four bedrooms at least in that penthouse of yours! I have a studio. No bedroom at all. Three hundred square feet. Besides, where else would they stay but with their big brother? We're a family, aren't we?"

Seb was sputtering.

"It won't be a problem," Vangie went on blithely. "Don't worry about it, Seb. You'll hardly know they're there."

The hell he wouldn't! Visions of panty hose drying, fingernail polish spilling, clutter everywhere hit him between the eyes. "Vangie! They can't—"

"Of course they can take care of themselves," she said, completely misunderstanding. "Don't fret. Go to your meeting. I'll talk to you later. And be sure to let me know if you hear from Dad."

And, bang, she was gone before he could say a word.

Seb glared at the phone, then slammed it down furiously. Blast Evangeline and her "normal" family fantasy anyway!

There was no way on earth he was going to share his penthouse with four of his sisters for an entire month! They'd drive him insane. Three twenty-year-olds and an eighteen-year-old—giggly, silly girl who, he knew from experience, would take over every square inch. He'd never get any work done. He'd never have a moment's peace.

He didn't mind footing the bills, but he was *not* having his space invaded! It didn't bear thinking about.

He gave a quick shuddering shake of his head, then snatched up his portfolio and stalked off to Max's office, where he would at least find an oasis of calm, of focus, of sanity, of engaging discussion with Max.

Gladys, Max's secretary, looked up from her computer and gave him a bright smile. "He's not here."

"Not here?" Seb frowned. "Why not? We've got a meeting."

Besides, it didn't make sense. Max was always here, except when he was on a site. And he never double scheduled. He was far too organized.

"I'm sure he'll be along. He's probably stuck in traffic."
Gladys gave Seb a bright smile. "I'll ring you when he gets here
if you'd like."

"Is he...on-site?"

"No. He's on his way back from the harbor."

"The harbor?" Seb frowned. He didn't remember Max having
a project down there, and he knew Max's projects.

Max was—had been ever since Seb had come to work for
him—his role model. Max Grosvenor was utterly reliable. A
paragon, in fact. Hardworking, focused, brilliant. Max was the
man he wanted to become, the father figure he'd never had.

Philip couldn't be bothered to turn up when he said he would,
but if Max wasn't here at—Seb glanced at his watch again—five
past three in the afternoon when he was the one who'd scheduled
the meeting, something was wrong.

"Is he all right?"

"Couldn't be better, I'd say." Gladys said cheerfully. Though
only ten or so years older than her boss, she doted on him like a
mother hen—not that Max ever noticed. "He's just been on a bit
of an outing."

Seb's brows drew down. *Outing?* Max? Max didn't do "outings."
But maybe Gladys had said "meeting" and he had misheard.

"I'm sure he'll be along shortly." Even as she spoke, the phone
on her desk rang. Raising a finger as if to say, wait, Gladys
answered it. "Mr. Grosvenor's office." The smile that creased her
face told Seb who it was.

He tapped his portfolio against his palm, watching as Gladys
listened, then nodded. "Indeed he is," she said into the phone.
"Right here waiting. Oh—" she glanced Seb's way, then smiled
"—I'm sure he'll live. Yes, Max. Yes, I'll tell him."

She hung up and, still smiling, looked up at Seb. "He's just come
into the parking garage. He says to go right in and wait if you want."

"Right. I'll do that." He must have misunderstood. She must
have said "meeting." Max must have had a new project come up.

"Thanks, Gladys." With a smile, Seb stepped past her and opened the door to Max's office.

It was always a jolt to walk into Max's office on a clear sunny day. Even when you were expecting it, the view was breathtaking.

Seb's own office, nearly as big and airy as Max's own, looked out to the north. He could sit at his desk and see up the coast. And if he shifted in his chair, he could watch the ferry crossing the water.

But Max could see paradise. Across the water, the Cascades spiked their way along the peninsula. A bevy of sailboats skimmed over the sound. And to the south the majesty of Mount Rainier loomed, looking almost close enough to touch.

The first time Seb had seen the view from Max's windows, he'd stopped dead, his eyes widening. "I don't see how you get any work done."

Max had shrugged. "You get used to it."

But now he stood and stared at the grandeur of Rainier for a long moment, Seb wasn't sure he ever would. And the memory of his first glimpse reminded him that when he'd first come out to the Pacific Northwest, he'd vowed to climb Rainier.

He never had. There hadn't been time.

Work had always been a bigger, more tempting mountain to climb. And there had always been more peaks, bigger peaks, tougher ones. And he'd relished the challenge, determined to prove himself. To make a name for himself. And make his own fortune to go with it.

The family had a fortune, of course. The hotel empire that Philip Savas oversaw guaranteed that. In another family, that fortune and those connections could have smoothed the way for a budding young architect. It hadn't. In fact, Seb doubted his father even knew what he did for a living, much less had ever wanted to encourage him.

Philip didn't care. He owned buildings, he didn't create them. And he had no interest in Seb's desire to.

The one time they'd discussed his future, when Seb was eighteen, Philip had said, "We can start you out in Hong Kong, I think."

And Seb had said, "What?"

"You need to get a taste of the whole business from the ground up, for when you come to work for us," Philip had said, as if it were a given.

When Seb had said, "I'm not," Philip had raised his brows, given his eldest son a long disapproving stare, then turned on his heel and walked out of the room.

End of discussion.

Seb would have said it was the end of the relationship, except they hadn't had much of one before that, either.

At least Philip's indifference had provided a wonderful incentive to do things his way, to make his own mark.

And standing here, in Max's office, feeling the cool spare elegance of his surroundings and admiring his spectacular view—which also happened to include over thirty buildings Grosvenor Design had been responsible for creating—Seb felt that surge of determination all over again.

He opened his portfolio and began laying out further sketches he'd done so they could jump right into things, when the door burst open and Max strode in.

Seb glanced up—and stared. "Max?"

Well, it was Max, of course. There was no mistaking the tall, lithe, angular body, the lean hawkish face, salt-and-pepper hair and the broad grin.

But where was the tie? The long-sleeved button-down oxford cloth shirt? The shiny black dress shoes? Max's uniform, in other words. The clothes Seb had seen Max Grosvenor wear every workday for the past ten years.

"You'll be more professional if you look professional," Max had said to Seb when he'd hired him. "Remember that."

Seb had. He was wearing his own version of the Grosvenor

Design uniform—navy slacks, long-sleeved grey-and-white pin-stripe shirt and toning tie—right now.

Max, on the other hand, was clad in a pair of faded jeans and a dark-blue windbreaker over a much-washed formerly gold sweatshirt with University of Washington on its chest in flaky white letters. His hair was windblown and his sockless feet were stuffed into a pair of rather new deck shoes. "Sorry I'm late," he said briskly. "Went sailing."

Seb had to consciously shut his mouth. Sailing? *Max?*

Well, of course thousands of people did—even on weekdays—but not Max Grosvenor. Max Grosvenor was a workaholic.

Now Max shucked his jacket and took a large design portfolio out of the cabinet. "I would have gone home to change, but I'd told you three. So—" he shrugged cheerfully "—here I am."

Seb was still nonplussed. A little confused. He could understand it if it had been a meeting. Even a meeting on a sailboat. And admittedly stranger things had happened. But he didn't ask.

And Max was all business now, despite his apparel. He opened the portfolio to their design for Blake-Carmody. "We got it," he said with a grin and a thumbs-up.

And Seb grinned, too, delighted that all their hard work had paid off.

"We went over it all while you were down in Reno," Max went on. "I brought along a couple of project people as well. Hope you don't mind, but time was of the essence."

"No. Not at all." Seb understood completely. While he had done considerable work on the project, Max was the president of the company.

And no one else could have gone to Reno in Seb's place. That medical complex project there was all his.

Max nodded. "Of course not. Good man." Still smiling, he dropped into the leather chair behind his desk and folded his arms behind his head, then nodded at the other chair for Seb to take a seat, too. "I was sure you'd understand. And I told Carmody a lot of the work was yours."

Seb settled into the other chair. "Thanks." He was glad to hear it, particularly because then Carmody would understand that Max wasn't solely responsible for the work and he wouldn't feel as if they were being fobbed off on an inferior when Seb took over.

Max dropped his arms and leaned forward, resting his forearms on his thighs as he locked his fingers together and said earnestly. "So I hope you won't feel cut out if I see this through myself."

Seb blinked.

"I know we'd talked about you taking it over," Max went on. "But you've been in Reno a lot. And you've still got a finger or two in Fogerty's project and the Hayes Building. Right?"

"Right." But that didn't mean he wouldn't be willing to work even harder to do Carmody-Blake.

Max nodded happily. "Exactly. And you'll have more time to run the bid on the school in Kent this way," he went on. "They were really impressed with your ideas."

Seb made an inarticulate sound at that point, hoping it sounded as if he was pleased with the compliment. It *was* a compliment. It was just—he'd really wanted the Blake-Carmody project.

He had no right to be disappointed, really. Logically he knew that. Yes, he'd been invited to share his ideas for the project, and yes, Max had taken them seriously. They'd even discussed the possibility of him taking over as head architect on the job. But while it had been unspoken, it had never been official.

And he could understand why Max would enjoy overseeing a plum job like this one. It was just that over the past couple of months Max had been talking about "stepping back" and "taking it easy."

And hell, he'd just come in from *sailing,* hadn't he?

"I knew you'd understand. Rodriguez is going to boss the office space side of it. Chang's doing the shops," Max went on.

That made sense. Frank Rodriguez and Danny Chang had also contributed to the portfolio with ideas that reflected their specialities. Seb nodded.

"And I've asked Neely to take charge of the living spaces."

"*What!*" Seb sat up straight. "*Neely Robson?*"

All of a sudden it didn't sound simply like Max keeping the plum job for himself. It sounded like—

Seb shook his head as if he were hearing things. "You can't be serious."

At his tone, Max stiffened abruptly. "I'm perfectly serious."

"But she's not experienced enough! She's been here, what? Six months? She's green."

"She's won awards. She got the Balthus Grant."

"She draws pretty pictures." All warm cozy stuff. She might as well be an interior decorator, Seb thought.

He'd only worked with Neely Robson one time—and that had been merely at the discussion stage in the first month she was there. It hadn't gone well. He'd thought her ideas were fluff and had said so. She had been of the opinion that he only wanted to build skyscrapers that were phallic symbols and had said that.

To say they hadn't hit it off was an understatement.

"The clients like her."

You like her, Seb wanted to say. *You like her curve body and her long honey colored hair and her luscious lips that curved into dimpled smiles.* But fortunately he clamped his teeth together before any of those words got past his lips.

"She's good at what she does," Max said mildly. He leaned back in his chair and steepled his fingers in front of his mouth, a smile playing on his lips as if he were thinking about something very different than designing buildings.

And what exactly has she been doing with you? Seb wondered acidly. But he had the brains not to say that, either.

Still he had to say something. It wasn't as if he hadn't noticed Neely Robson's appeal to his boss over the past couple of months. She was an attractive woman. No question about it. A man would have to be dead not to notice.

But the firm was big enough that she hadn't really come to Max's notice until she'd won that damned award in February. Then he'd invited her to work on the hospital addition.

Since then Max had paid more and more attention to her.

Seb couldn't count the number of times he had noticed her coming out of Max's office or the multitude of times in the last couple of months he'd heard her name on Max's lips. And he'd certainly seen Max's gaze linger on her in staff meetings.

He hadn't worried. Max wasn't Philip Savas, he'd told himself. Max was single-minded, determined, professional. If anyone was the poster boy for workaholics, it was Max.

There was no way Max Grosvenor was going to let himself be seduced by a pretty face. He was fifty-two years old, and no woman had trapped him into matrimony yet, had she?

Seb supposed there was always a first time. And Max could be ripe for a midlife crisis. He'd gone *sailing,* for crying out loud!

"I just mean she doesn't have a lot of expertise with condos as a part of multi-use buildings and—"

"You don't have to worry about her expertise. I'll be working closely with her," Max said now. "And if she's green, well, she'll learn. I think I can help her out." He raised a brow. "Don't you agree?"

Seb gritted his teeth so hard his jaw ached. "Of course," he said stiffly.

Max grinned cheerfully. "She's got a lot on the ball, Seb. Very creative. You should get to know her."

"I know her," Seb said shortly.

Max laughed. "Not the way I do. Come sailing with us next time, why don't you?"

"Next— You went sailing with—" He didn't finish the sentence so appalled—and disbelieving—was he at the prospect. Max and Neely Robson had spent the afternoon sailing? Dear

God, yes, he must be having a midlife crisis. That was the sort of thing Philip Savas would do, but not Max Grosvenor.

"She's not a bad little sailor." Max grinned.

"Isn't she?" Seb hauled himself to his feet and picked up his portfolio. "I'm glad to hear it," he said flatly. "But I still think you're making a mistake."

Max's smile faded. He stared out the window at Mount Rainier for a long moment, though whether he saw it Seb had no idea. Finally he brought his eyes back to meet Seb's.

"It wouldn't be the first mistake I've ever made," he said quietly. "I appreciate your concern." He met Seb's gaze squarely. "But I don't think I'm making a mistake this time."

Their gazes locked. Seb wanted to tell him how wrong he was, how he'd seen it over and over and over from his own father.

He gave his head a little shake but then just nodded. "I'll just be getting back to work then, if you don't have anything else to discuss."

Max gave a wave of his hand. "No, nothing else. I just wanted to let you know about Blake-Carmody in person. Seemed tactless to leave it on your phone. And it's no disrespect to you, Seb, my taking this on. It's just—this is one I want to do."

With Neely Robson.

He didn't say it. He didn't have to.

"Of course," Seb said tightly.

He had the door open when Max's voice came from behind him. "You should take a little time off yourself, Seb. All work and no play—you know the saying."

Seb did. But he didn't want to hear it from Max Grosvenor. He shut the door wordlessly as he went out.

"There now, isn't it lovely?" Gladys looked up and sighed happily.

Seb frowned. "Sorry?"

"Max," she said with a sappy maternal smile. "It's lovely he's finally getting a life."

* * *

If Max was finally getting a life, Seb didn't envy him.

Life—the "relationship" sort—as Seb knew from a lifetime of experience, was messy, unpredictable and fraught with chaos. That Max, the most focused of men, should be tempted by it, simply meant he was deep in a midlife crisis.

And with Neely Robson—a woman half his age, for God's sake! It was a disaster waiting to happen.

Max had always had what Seb thought was an ideal life. Satisfaction through work, through creating magnificent buildings, a life of order, clear and controllable. Not messy, unpredictable and tangled.

If Max was getting a life, Seb pitied him. He was doomed to disappointment.

Seb shook his head, then shoved away the thought of Max's idiocy and tried to concentrate on the Kent school project.

It was after six. He could have quit. But why? There was work to do here and certainly no reason to go home.

Talking about messy and uncontrollable, by now he was sure his penthouse condo would be teeming with half sisters. There would be panty hose in all the bathrooms, cell phones ringing at every minute, toast crumbs and marmalade on the countertops, half-eaten yogurts in the refrigerator and bridal magazines littering every horizontal surface.

Even worse they would all be talking at once—about the wedding, about Evangeline and Garrett, about how perfect it all was, about how they were going to live happily ever after, about how everyone should live happily ever after. And then they would begin comparing their own love lives.

And speculating about his.

Ever since they'd been in junior high school his sisters had been pestering him about the women in his life. Who was he dating? Was it serious? Did he love her?

Love! Titter, titter. Giggle, giggle.

It made Seb's jaw muscles twitch every time he thought about it.

He didn't have a love life. Didn't intend to have one. Not one like they meant, anyway—not that he could get it through their romantic fluffy-brained heads.

He had needs, of course. Hormones. Testosterone, for God's sake. He was a red-blooded male with all the right instincts. But that didn't mean marriage or happily ever after.

And it certainly didn't mean he believed in fairy tales.

On the contrary, he believed in giving his hormones exactly what they wanted in a sane, sensible fashion. And he had done so over the years through a series of discreet liaisons with women who wanted exactly what he did. No more, no less.

And if his last discreet liaison had ended a few months ago because the pretty blonde software engineer with whom he'd been satisfying those hormones had taken a job in Philly just after the first of the year, that simply meant he needed to find another woman to take her place.

It didn't mean he had to get a love life or get serious.

But his sisters thought he should. And they were never hesitant to say so.

And since Evangeline had foisted them on him for the next month—and he knew he wasn't going to be able to turf them out—they would feel entitled to express their opinions. At length.

God help him.

He needed a bolt hole, a bachelor pad. A tiny hideaway of his own—just for the month—where none of them could find him. He could appear and be big brotherly when the mood suited him, but generally he could play "least in sight."

He toyed with the idea of moving into the empty studio apartment in the building he'd bought two years ago. It was tempting. But it was only three blocks from where he lived. And Vangie knew about it. They'd all know about it if he went there.

It wouldn't be a bolt hole for long.

He'd like to stick them there, but that would never work. One room plus one bathroom and the four of them? It didn't bear thinking about.

Maybe he could buy a futon for his office and sleep here. A few months ago Max would have applauded the idea. Now, in his new "isn't playing hooky wonderful?" mode, he would have a fit.

But damn it, Seb wasn't having a midlife crisis. And if he wanted to work 24-7 why shouldn't he? At least here at the office, he could still focus.

Deliberately Seb shoved the thought away and focused once more on the Kent school designs. Almost everyone else had gone home now. It was close to six-thirty. Max had breezed out half an hour ago.

He'd stuck his head in on his way to the elevator. "Still here? It's Friday night. No hot date?"

Seb just looked at him.

Max grinned and shook his head. "Learn from me, man. There's more to life than work."

Like hot dates with a woman half his age? Seb sucked in his cheeks. "I have some work to do for Reno, then I want to think a bit about the Kent project."

Max gave him a wry look that said he recognized the guilt being offered him, but then, pure Max, he shrugged it off. "Up to you." He started away, then returned to stick his head round the door again. "We're going sailing on Sunday. Come along?"

Oh, yes. That was exactly how Seb wanted to spend his Sunday—watching Max make a fool of himself over Neely Robson—and watching Neely Robson gloat. Seb gritted his teeth. "Thanks, but I'm busy. My sisters are in town."

If he was stuck with them, the least they could do was be useful.

Max nodded. "Right. You have a big family. I always forget that."

Seb wished he could.

"Lucky you. I'm glad you'll have some distraction," Max said. "You won't make the same mistake I did."

No, he wouldn't! There was no way on earth Seb was going to go all ga-ga over an unsuitable conniving woman. "Have fun," Seb said drily.

Max flashed him a grin. "I intend to."

And he sauntered away. Whistling, for God's sake!

Seb thrust his fingers through his hair and kneaded his scalp and tried to focus again.

He tried for another half an hour after Max left. But his stomach began growling, and he needed to get something to eat. At least he didn't have to go home for that. He could get takeaway, bring it back here, stay and work until it was time to go to bed.

Like the triplets *ever* went to bed.

He shoved back his chair and grabbed his suit jacket off the back of his chair, then stepped out into the common room.

There was only one other light still on. Four doors down in Frank Rodriguez's office. Frank, who was doing the Blake-Carmody office space, would be happily burning the midnight oil. And as he walked toward the office on his way to the elevator, he could hear Frank and Danny Chang in deep conversation.

Seb felt a prick of envy, then tamped it down. He didn't want Frank's job. Or Danny's. And it wasn't their fault he hadn't got the job he did want.

"Can't help you," he heard Danny Chang say. "Wish I could." He stepped out of Frank's office, then paused in the doorway and turned back. "I thought you had it sold."

"So did I," Frank's tone was glum. "Cath is going to freak when she finds out the deal fell through. We want this house. How the hell am I going to put the down payment on the house if I don't have it?"

Danny shrugged. "If I hear of anyone who wants one, I'll send 'em your way." He turned to go, then stopped and did a double take at the sight of Seb. "Hey, wanna buy a houseboat?"

Houseboat?

Did he want to buy a…*houseboat?*

Any other day Seb would have laughed. Today as the words registered, he found himself saying cautiously, curiously, "What sort of houseboat? Where?"

Danny and Frank exchanged glances.

Then Frank got up from behind his desk and came to the door of his office. "Not big. You probably wouldn't want it. Two bedrooms. One bath. Pretty small really. On the east side of Lake Union. Bought it after I'd been here a year. I love it. But Cath—we're getting married—and Cath doesn't. She says she's not into *Sleepless in Seattle.*"

Seb had no idea what he meant. He wasn't into chick flicks. But a houseboat… "Tell me more."

Frank's eyes widened in surprise. And then, apparently deciding Seb was serious, he ticked off its virtues. "It's perfectly functional. Fifty-odd years old, but it's been well cared for. Pretty quiet place. Right at the end of the dock. Great views, obviously. My tenant was going to buy it, but the financing fell through. I just got the call."

"Tenant?"

Frank shrugged. "I rent out the other bedroom. Helps with the payments. But nothing's going to help with this," he said grimly. "We're not going to have the money for the down payment and we're going to lose the house."

And tenants could be moved. "How much do you want for it?"

Frank blinked. "Seriously?"

"I'm asking, aren't I?"

"Oh! Well, um…" Frank looked a bit dazed as he spit out a figure.

Not a bargain. But what price did you put on peace? Sanity. A lack of clutter and giggles and panty hose? Besides, he could always sell it.

Seb nodded. "I'll write you a check."

CHAPTER TWO

IT WAS perfect.

Seb could see the houseboat as he came down the hill. It sat at the end of the dock. Other houseboats were moored on either side, but his was right at the end—two stories high of weathered grey wood and very crisp white trim, it looked snug and welcoming, just as Frank had said it would be.

As it was backlit by the setting sun, Seb couldn't see all the details. But from what he could discern, it was the bolt hole of his dreams.

He couldn't have made a better decision, Seb thought as he parked his car, then grabbed two of the duffel bags he'd packed and headed down the dock. He felt alive somehow, energized, actually smiling in anticipation.

Sure, it was a lot of money to pay for a month's bolt hole. But what else was he doing with his money besides footing the wedding bill for his sister, paying college tuition for all of his sundry siblings and providing tummy tucks and face-lifts for his father's ex-wives?

Besides, Frank had assured him, a houseboat was an eminently resalable item. His urgency to sell only had to do with his impending marriage and baby. He was sure his tenant would buy it whenever Seb wanted out, presuming the financing worked out then. And if not, there would be plenty of other interested buyers.

So, when—*if*—Seb wanted to sell, he might even make a profit.

But it wasn't the profit that interested him now. It was the peace and quiet. The solitude.

If he'd needed any convincing that he'd done the right thing by his impulse down payment and promise to get the financing tomorrow, walking into his penthouse tonight had done it.

The panty hose were already everywhere. So were the crumbs and the sticky marmalade plates. The cell phones shrilled and his sisters giggled. There they were talking—all of them at once—and throwing their arms around him, hugging him, getting him sticky, too.

He had been prepared for that.

But he'd forgotten the music, the television, the shouting over each other to be heard. He'd forgotten the smells. The sickly sweet shampoos, conditioners, hair sprays, gels, mousses, not to mention umpteen kinds of perfume actually supposed to have fragrances.

His whole apartment had smelled like a bordello.

If he'd thought for one second he'd been wrong to jump at Frank's houseboat, those few minutes had convinced him he'd done exactly the right thing. He could hardly wait to escape.

His sisters had been appalled when he'd slipped out of their embraces and headed for his bedroom to pack.

"You've got a trip? Now?"

"Where are you going?"

"When are you coming back?"

They'd followed him into his room. He could see makeup bottles scattered on the countertop through the door to his bathroom.

"I'm just giving you some space," he said. "And trusting you with mine," he added with his best severe older brother glower. It went from them to the open door of the bathroom where there were also wet towels on the floor. Then it went back to them. They smiled contritely.

"Keep things clean," he said. "Pick up after yourselves. I've got work to do and I need to focus."

"We won't be any trouble," they vowed in unison, heads bobbing.

Seb had smiled at that. Then he'd gathered up the few things he was sure he would need or that he really didn't want them to break—like his grandfather's old violin—and patted their heads.

"I'll be back and take you to dinner on Sunday," he promised.

As he left, Jenna borrowed money to pay the pizza delivery man.

"Sure you won't change your mind, Seb?" she'd said, forgetting to give him the change.

Seb had shaken his head. "No."

But now, as his stomach rumbled on his way down the dock, he wished he'd at least thought to snatch one of the pizzas.

No matter. He'd grab something after he settled in—and dealt with Frank's tenant. A guy who rented a room on a houseboat ought to be delighted to be offered a studio apartment rent free. And maybe by the time Seb was ready to sell, he'd have his finances in order and could get a loan.

Seb found himself whistling just like Max as he stepped aboard his houseboat and turned the key in the front door lock.

"Home sweet home," he murmured, and pushed open the door and stepped into a small foyer with a staircase leading up to the second floor on one side and bookshelves and a door on the other. Straight ahead, down a hallway he glimpsed the setting sun through the window. It drew him on. So did the music he heard.

Unlike the cacophonous racket he'd left behind with his sisters, this was a Bach minuet, light and lilting, rhythmic, orderly.

The lingering tension in Seb's shoulders eased. He'd wondered how he would convince Frank's tenant that he needed to move. The Bach reassured him. A tenant who played Bach would see the logic and good sense in Seb's offer to put him up rent free.

He made his way down the hallway and into an open living area and stopped stock-still at the sight of a rabbit hutch—complete with two rabbits—on a window seat. There was an aquarium on the bar that separated the kitchen area from the rest of the room. There were three half-grown kittens wrestling on the floor and one attempting to clamber up a cardboard box that had been strategically placed to keep it inside while the door to the deck beyond could be left open.

But none of it was quite as astonishing as the sight of a pair of long bare very female legs halfway up a ladder out on the deck.

"You're back?" the female said, apparently having heard Seb shutting the door. "This is way too soon. Go away and come back in half an hour."

Seb didn't move. Just stared at the legs. Felt wholly masculine interest at the same time he felt stirrings of unease.

His tenant was *female?*

And Frank hadn't bothered to mention it?

Well, maybe to Frank it hadn't made any difference. He had been spending his time at his fiancée's afterall.

"Cody?" The woman's voice said when Seb didn't reply. "Did you hear me? I said, Go away."

Seb cleared his throat. "I'm not Cody," he said, grateful his voice didn't croak as his eyes were still glued to those amazing legs.

"Not…?" Bare feet moved down the ladder one rung at a time until the woman could hook her arm around one side of the ladder and swung her head down so that she could see him.

Seb stared, transfixed.

Neely Robson?

No. Impossible.

Seb shut his eyes. It was just that his irritating meeting with Max had had the effect of imprinting her on his brain.

When he opened them again he would, of course, see some other stunningly gorgeous woman with dark honey-colored hair and legs a mile long.

He opened them again.

It was Neely Robson.

They stared at each other.

And then, almost in slow motion, she straightened up again

so he could no longer see her face—only her legs—and for an instant he could tell himself that he'd imagined it.

Then slowly those amazing legs descended the ladder and she came to stare in the open doorway at him, the paintbrush in one hand as she swiped her hair away from her face with the other.

"Mr. Savas," she said politely in that slightly husky oh-so-provocative voice.

Did she call Max "Mr. Grosvenor"? Seb wondered acidly.

"Ms. Robson," he replied curtly, keeping his gaze resolutely away from her long bare legs, though seeing her blowsy and barely buttoned above the waist wasn't entirely settling.

"I'm sorry. I wasn't expecting—I thought you were Cody with Harm." There was a flush across her cheeks and she suddenly looked confused.

Seb shook his head, not sure what she was talking about and feeling confused himself.

"My dog. Harmony. That's his name. Well, not really. But it sounds better. His name is Harm. As in, 'he does more harm than good.'" Her words tumbled out quickly. "The boy down the dock took him for a walk. I thought you were them coming back and I'm not done painting yet."

Seb had never heard Neely Robson babble before and he would have found it entertaining under other circumstances. Now he raised a brow and she stopped abruptly.

"Never mind," she said. "You're looking for Frank."

"No."

She blinked. "No?" A pause. "Then…why are you—?" She looked him in the eyes, then her gaze traveled down and he saw when it lit on his bags. Her frown deepened.

Damn, he wished he could enjoy this more. Wished he had been prepared. Wished he were a lot less shocked than she was by the turn of events.

No matter. What was done was done. And Neely Robson was on her way out.

"Sorry to disappoint you, Ms. Robson," he drawled. "I've already seen Frank. Now I'm moving in."

"*What?*" The color drained from her face. Her tone was outraged.

Seb did enjoy that. He smiled thinly. "If you're the 'tenant,' Ms. Robson, you have a new landlord. Me."

She was hearing things.

Neely used to tell her mother that would happen.

"I'll go deaf if you keep playing that music so loud," she used to say all the time she was growing up with hard rock at a hundred decibels blaring in her ears while her mother made jewelry out of old seeds and twigs.

She was probably the only child in the history of the world who had a parent more likely to shatter her eardrums than to wait for Neely to do it herself.

Lara—her mother had never wanted to be called Mom or Mother. "Do I look like somebody's mother?" she would challenge anyone who dared—had always laughed at her.

But apparently, Neely thought now, staring in dismay at the man in her living room, she had been right.

It was appalling enough to have God's gift to long-sleeved dress shirts, Sebastian Savas, standing in her living room looking down his nose at her, but to think she heard him say he was moving in and that he was her landlord. Well, that simply didn't bear contemplating.

"I beg your pardon," she said, enunciating clearly so that he would, too, and she could figure out what he really said. "What did you say?"

"I bought the houseboat."

Neely felt her knees wobble. She braced a hand on the doorjamb to make sure she didn't topple right over.

"No."

"Oh, yes." And he bared his teeth in what she supposed was

intended to be smile. Or a smirk. "*This* houseboat," he clarified, just in case she thought he meant another one. "I'm moving in."

There was no consolation at all in discovering her hearing was just fine. Neely stared at him, aghast, disbelieving even in the face of evidence, then shook her head because it couldn't be true. "You're mistaken. *I'm* buying the houseboat. It's *mine*."

"Sadly…for you—" Sebastian stressed these last two words, because it was, quite apparently, not sad for him at all "—it's not. Not yours, I mean. Frank sold it to me a couple of hours ago."

"He can't! He wouldn't! We had a deal."

Sebastian shrugged. "It fell through."

She stared at him, feeling as if she'd just caught a lead basketball in the stomach, feeling exactly the way she always had whenever Lara had told her they were moving. Again. And again. And again.

"You don't know that," she said slowly, setting down the paintbrush and wrapping her arms across her chest. But even as she said the words, she felt an awful sense of foreboding.

"Personally, no, I don't," Sebastian said easily. "But Frank knew. He said someone called Gregory called him. A mortgage broker, I assume?"

The sense of foreboding wasn't a sense any longer. It was reality. Neely nodded. "A friend of Frank's." Her fingernails dug into the flesh of her upper arms. "He promised to find a loan for me."

"Yes, well, apparently it didn't work out."

"There are other places to look," Neely insisted urgently. "Other lenders."

Sebastian nodded. There wasn't a flicker of sympathy in his gaze. "No doubt. But Frank couldn't wait. Something about a down payment on a house? A wedding? A baby on the way? He was pretty stressed." Something else Mr. Coldhearted Savas couldn't possibly care about.

And why should he?

It had all worked out perfectly for him.

Now he set his duffel bag on the floor and his garment bag on the sofa, then turned toward the door.

"What are you doing?" she demanded shrilly, clambering over the big cardboard box and coming after him.

"Going back for more of my things. Want to help?" She couldn't see his face, but she had no trouble imagining the smirk on his lips.

He didn't wait for a reply. He left.

And she steamed. She grabbed her mobile phone off the table on the deck and punched in Frank's number.

He wasn't answering.

"Coward," she muttered.

"Are you talking to me?" Sebastian Savas came back in carrying two big boxes and set them on the coffee table. *Her* coffee table!

"That's mine," she snapped.

He followed her gaze to the table in question. "I beg your pardon. Frank said he was leaving some furniture."

"Not that table," Neely said, knowing she was being petty. Not caring.

"Right." He picked up the boxes and set them beside it on the floor. "It is my floor," he said, making her feel about two inches high—until he gave her another one of those smiles and walked out again.

Neely wanted to scream as she watched him return with another big box and deliberately set it beside the others on the floor. *His* floor.

"I can't believe you bought it," Neely muttered, still fuming.

"I can't, either," Sebastian said so cheerfully that she wanted to smack him. "But it's perfect."

That comment actually surprised her. She would never have thought Sebastian Savas would consider a rather battered half-century-old houseboat perfect at all. She'd never seen his place, but Max had said he lived in a penthouse somewhere. What had happened to that?

"I can't imagine why you think so," she said acidly.

"But then, you don't know my circumstances, do you?" he said, hands on his hips as he stood surveying his domain.

"Did you get evicted?" Neely asked sweetly.

He gave her a stare hard enough to make her back up a step. She would need to watch her mouth if he really intended to stick around.

But the next instant she found herself saying, "Or maybe you ran away from home."

"Maybe I did," he agreed.

She blinked. "Yeah, sure. Tell me, why did you do it?"

"Danny asked if I wanted to buy a houseboat."

"And you just thought, 'Sure why not?' and whipped out your checkbook and said, 'I'll take it'?"

"Something like that."

She didn't believe a word of it. "Get real."

He just shrugged.

She hated that about him—that superior cool detachment, that nothing-gets-to-me disdain. At work they called him The Iceman behind his back. They might have called him Iceman to his face for all he'd care.

She watched him open one of the boxes, remove some books and casually begin taking over the bookshelves. She sucked in her breath.

Sebastian turned and glanced her way. "What? No protest? Are the shelves mine, then?"

"As they're built in, it seems they are," Neely said through her teeth. "But as the renter I'm entitled to use some of the space."

"Ah, yes. Your rent."

"It's locked in—the amount," she said firmly, in case he decided to triple it. Or worse. "On my lease."

He didn't reply, just said, "Shall I measure and divide the space, then? To be sure you're getting your fair share?"

"I think we can work it out," Neely muttered, glowering at him as he straightened again, hating the six feet, two inches of hard, lean, dark masculinity taking over her space and scoring her with assessing looks from his piercing green eyes.

They were gorgeous eyes—such a pale green at contrast with his olive complexion and thick black hair. They made his strong, handsome, almost hawkish face even more memorable— and appealing.

"Who's he? He's hot," all the temp girls at the office said when they first caught a glimpse him. "I'll take him for *my* boss."

But once they'd worked for him, they changed their minds.

Sebastian Savas had a reputation for being exacting, demanding and unflappable. Absolutely businesslike. And completely cold.

To a woman, the fools flirted with him, batted their lashes at him, simpered and brought him endless cups of coffee in the hope that he would: speak to them, date them, marry them.

He barely noticed them.

As far as Neely could tell, he only noticed buildings—the taller and pointier the better.

A fact which she had once mentioned to him. Had wondered aloud if his fascination might be a means of overcompensation. But only because he'd dismissed her sketches saying they weren't building doll houses for Barbie!

No, they weren't. They were designing offices for a trendy women's magazine publisher whose signature color was hot pink. But Sebastian hadn't understood that. He'd just dismissed her attempt to get the color in the interior lines of the offices.

She hadn't had anything to do with him since.

Didn't want to.

He was Max's right-hand man and Max thought he was terrific. He'd sung Sebastian's praises often enough. But they were pretty much two of a kind, so why wouldn't Max think so?

"You'll like him when you get to know him," Max had promised.

Neely didn't think so. And she had no wish to get to know him at all.

She had no use for workaholic men. Twenty-six years ago, a

workaholic man hadn't married her pregnant mother. Not that her mother had been, at the time, the marrying kind.

But all of that was irrelevant at the moment.

What was relevant right now was finding out exactly what sort of game Mr. Iceman Savas was playing.

"So you're saying you just whipped out your checkbook to save Frank's bacon?" She pressed.

"I did us both a favor. He wanted to sell. I wanted to buy. We made a deal. Simple."

It wasn't simple at all. Not to her. Neely opened her mouth to argue further with him, but knew there was no point.

Arguing wasn't going to change anything. The loan had fallen through. And to be honest, she'd always known it might. Her bank balance was promising, but not substantial, certainly nowhere close to what Sebastian Savas's was.

She'd only been earning good money since her graduation from university two and a half years ago. And a good chunk of that every month went to repay her student loans and provide a bit more ready cash for her mother. Lara, who had married finally when Neely was twelve, was now a widow with a limited pension and a small jewelry business. She was self-sufficient, but there were no extras—unless Neely provided them.

Buying the houseboat had been her dream. She'd loved it from the moment she'd rented a room from Frank six months ago. And she'd dared to hope, when he decided to give in to Cath's wishes and sell the houseboat, that she would have enough saved to qualify to buy it.

Apparently she hadn't. Yet.

And with time of the essence, Frank had been unable to wait and had taken the easy way out.

The Sebastian Savas way out.

"Speaking of deals, I have a deal for you, Ms. Robson," Sebastian said now. He was standing there holding a stack of books in his hands, regarding her steadily with his green gaze.

"Deal?" Neely said, suddenly hopeful. "You'll sell to me?"

Would he really? After all the bad things she'd thought about him? After the less-than-pleasant things she'd *said* to him?

He shook his head. "No, but I've got a place you can go."

She felt punched in the gut again. So much for pipe dreams.

"There's a vacant studio apartment in a building I own." He looked at her expectantly, as if he thought she would jump for joy at the prospect. "You can have it rent-free for six months."

She shook her head. "I'm not going anywhere."

His brows drew down. "You have to. I'm moving in." He hefted the books to make his point.

"Bully for you."

He stared at her. The green gaze grew icier than ever. "So you're saying you want to share?" His voice was silky with innuendo and hard with challenge.

Neely shrugged with all the indifference she could muster. She hoped it was an Oscarworthy performance.

"Well, I don't want to, but if you're moving in, apparently we are." She jerked her head toward the stairs. "Your bedroom is the one to the right at the top. It's smaller than mine, but it has the better view. Enjoy it."

She didn't wait to hear his reply to that. She didn't want to know. Besides, she needed to get away from him before she threw her paintbrush at him—or something worse.

So she climbed back over the cardboard box, picked up the paintbrush, scaled the ladder and began slapping paint on the wall again. In her head—and heart—she was slapping Sebastian Savas.

If she expected him to turn and leave, she was out of luck.

No big surprise there.

He didn't head up the stairs, either. Instead he set the books on the shelf, then moved the box out of the doorway and came after her out onto the narrow deck and leaned against the railing to stare up at her.

"The kittens will get out," she warned.

He ignored her and the kittens. "I don't want a roommate, Ms. Robson." His tone was flat and uncompromising. She'd heard it before—at the office.

"Neither do I," Neely said in an equally clipped tone. She dipped the paintbrush into the can and continued slapping the wall, not looking down, though she knew exactly where he was behind her.

The paint was a soft grey called "silver linings." When she'd bought it, she'd thought how appropriate it was, having a paint color that would reflect her journey—the hard road and eventual joyous return that had brought her back to her birthplace, to a job she loved and a houseboat she was going to call her own.

Now she thought that if there was a god of paint cans, it was very likely having a good laugh at her expense.

"Then you'll have to move," Sebastian said. "Understand that I'm not tossing you into the street. My offer is very fair, and the apartment is in a good location."

"No doubt. Not interested." Slap, slap.

She heard his breath hiss between his teeth. "Look, Ms. Robson," he began again in what she was sure were determinedly measured tones, "you don't seem to understand. Your staying here is not an option. You can take my offer of a very nice studio apartment for the next six months or you can simply pack up and leave. You can't stay here."

Neely turned her body slightly so she could look down over her shoulder at him in the twilight. He looked big and imposing even below her, and she was grateful for the ladder's height. "On the contrary, Mr. Savas," she said in measured tones of her own. "I certainly can stay here. I have a lease. As in a legally binding contract. An agreement," she added with saccharine sweetness. "In writing. Frank's Cath is an attorney. She wanted to be sure he had all his legal i's dotted and t's crossed. Ironclad, she said. I believe her. Just try to weasel out of it." The smile she gave him would have challenged the Cheshire cat's.

His jaw tightened. "Then I'll buy you out of it."

Neely shrugged. "Sell me the houseboat. I offered Frank good money."

"And couldn't come up with it, apparently."

Neely bristled. "I'm good for it. I have a good job, good prospects."

He snorted. She'd never heard so much derision in a single sound. Now it was her turn to frown. "What's that for?"

"Your prospects." His tone was disparaging. "Is that what you're calling Max these days? I'm sure he'll be delighted to hear it."

"Max?" Neely's jaw dropped as his meaning became clear. He thought she was...using Max?

She stared, openmouthed. Then abruptly she snapped her mouth shut. She'd have liked to tip the paint can over on his arrogant head.

At her silence he shrugged. "And I see you're not denying it."

"I most certainly am denying it!"

"Well, don't bother. Just because he's too blind to see what you're after doesn't mean the rest of us are."

Neely's fingers strangled the paintbrush. She wished they were strangling Sebastian Savas's strong muscular neck. "The rest of you?" she forced the words past her lips. "Who exactly?"

"Me for one. Gladys."

"Max's secretary thinks I'm out to use him?"

"Oh, she's delighted you're humanizing him." Sebastian sneered at her. "I can think of another word for it."

"You don't know what you're talking about," she told him frostily.

A sardonic brow lifted. "Don't I?"

"No, Mr. Savas, you don't. And you shouldn't presume." So saying, she wrenched around and set to painting again. Slap, slap, slap. God, she was furious at him! She was positively steaming.

"So, what's it going to take to shift you, Ms. Robson?" he persisted. "What's your price?"

Neely ignored him. The sun had almost set. She needed to turn on the light if she were going to actually see that she was accomplishing something. But then again, who cared? If this was Sebastian Savas's houseboat now, not hers, why should she bother to paint at all?

Because it *was* hers, damn it!

She was the one who had painted it, who had coddled it, who had taken care of it when Frank was more interested in just moving in with Cath. He'd *promised* her!

Maybe she should have taken Max up on his offer.

When it had become clear to him that he was never going to talk her out of her independence and into his glass and stone and cedar palace overlooking the sound, he'd said he would help her finance it.

Neely had refused, too stubborn, too proud to let him.

"No," she'd said firmly. "I appreciate the offer. Thank you. But I want to do it myself."

And look what it got her—out on her ear.

If Mr. Jump-to-Conclusions, Look-Down-His-Nose-At-Her Savas only knew Max had already offered, he'd blow a gasket. But then, obviously Sebastian thought he did know—everything. Pompous jerk.

He didn't even *want* her houseboat. Not really. She was sure of it. He had a use for it now, though she had no idea what. But ultimately he'd move back to his penthouse.

She set down the brush and deliberately turned to look down at him once more. "What's *your* price, Mr. Savas?"

"*My* price?" He looked startled.

But then his insolent gaze started at her bare feet and took its time sliding up the length of her legs, making her supremely aware of exactly what he seemed to be assessing.

Neely felt her cheeks begin to burn and she wanted to kick his smug face even as she waited for what would certainly be an unpleasant suggestion. And she had only herself to blame because she'd asked for it.

But then slowly he shook his head. "You don't have anything I'd want to buy, Ms. Robson."

Oh, God, she wanted to kick him.

But before she could react at all, Cody and Harm burst into the room as only thirteen-year-old boys and one-year-old bloodhounds can do. "We're back! Harm got in the mud and I need a towel and—"

Cody wasn't reckoning on a stranger on the boat. Harm loved strangers. Actually he loved everyone. There was no accounting for taste.

Still, in this case, Neely couldn't complain. One look at a man on the deck and Harm broke loose from Cody's grasp. Sebastian had moved the box to pursue her onto the deck. It wasn't keeping the kittens in the living room. And it certainly didn't stop Harm as he shot straight through the living room.

"Oh, dear," she said. "Hang on."

Too late.

A ninety-seven-pound missile of canine enthusiasm launched his joyful muddy self at Sebastian Savas—and sent them both straight over the railing into the water!

As much as Neely would have loved to stand there and laugh, it would be just her luck for Sebastian to be a nonswimmer. Bad enough that he would probably sue her and her dog for everything she might ever own.

She scrambled down the ladder as he sputtered to the surface, water streaming down his face. "Are you all right?"

She wished he would yell or shout or even threaten her. She wouldn't even mind if he tried to strangle her dog.

He didn't. Jaw set, he took the two strokes necessary to reach the side of the houseboat, then began to haul himself out of the water. He didn't say a word.

Neely watched with wary fascination, expecting to see steam coming off him, and supposing he would be entitled if it did. Two of the kittens were peering over the railing, leaning perilously close to falling in. Harm was dog-paddling cheerfully and grinning at her.

Staying well out of Sebastian's way as he clambered over the railing, Neely scooped up the kittens, then stuck them back in the living room and dragged the box in front of the open doorway again.

"I told you not to move the box," she pointed out to Sebastian as he dripped. "I'm, um, sorry," she added. Though it would have been more convincing if she'd been able to wipe the smile off her face.

Sebastian, of course, didn't acknowledge it. He turned to watch Harm paddling around the side of the houseboat to clamber up onto the dock.

"I'll go get 'im," Cody volunteered quickly, and darted out the front door to do so before anyone could blame him.

But Neely certainly wasn't blaming him. And Sebastian still didn't say anything.

She found it amazing that even dripping wet he could still look unflappable. The man really was inhuman.

And then he murmured, "More harm than good?" in a quiet reflective tone that made her blink. And blink again.

Was that a sense of humor?

She wasn't sure. "Er, yes." She laughed nervously. Probably it wasn't.

Sebastian nodded gravely. "Does he do it often?"

Her lips twitched. "Knock people in the water? More often than I'd like, actually. Mostly it's me, though. I've learned not to stand by the railing when he's excited. He's still a puppy. Just a year old." Was that sufficient excuse? Probably not.

"I am sorry," she said again, finally managing not to smile. She snagged up the last escapee kitten and clutched it in front of her as if it were a shield.

Green eyes met hers. "No, you're not."

Their gazes met again. And Neely remembered the first time they had confronted each other—over her "fluffy ideas" and his "phallic skyscrapers." Something had sizzled then. And Neely, feeling it, had darted away, telling herself it was irritation.

Of course there was irritation now. In spades.

But there was more. If there had been steam before, there certainly was now, as well as something hot and electric and very very intense that seemed to snap between them.

Neely felt an unaccountable urge to fling herself into the cold Lake Union water.

Deliberately she took a deep breath, then strove for a calm she didn't feel as she met his gaze squarely and said, "You're right. I'm not."

And who knows how long they might have stood there, gazes dueling, heat and awareness crackling, if Cody hadn't returned with Harm just then?

"Got 'im. At least he's not muddy anymore." Cody looked hopefully at Neely, then his gaze went straight to Sebastian.

Neely went in and took the dog by the collar. "Thanks," she said to Cody. But he barely seemed to notice her. He was craning his neck to see past her toward the man still dripping on the deck.

"Who's he?" he asked.

"A man I work with."

"Your new neighbor," Sebastian said firmly, coming in the door.

Cody's eyes widened and he looked a bit worried as he turned for confirmation to Neely. "Really? Where d'you live?"

"Here."

That did make Cody's eyes bug. "With Neely?"

"No!" they both said in unison.

"I'm not moving," Neely said flatly.

Sebastian's jaw tightened.

Cody looked from one to the other nervously. "I got homework," he said. "Math. Lots of it. Gotta go." And he darted out the door before either of them could say a word.

In the silence that followed his departure, Harm shook himself vigorously, getting Neely almost as wet as Sebastian. She hauled the dog into the kitchen and began to dry him.

Sebastian came after her, loomed over her, still dripping. "I'm not leaving," he told her.

Neely looked up and met his stony gaze. "Neither am I."

"I own this boat."

She took a careful breath. "And I have a lease to rent a room on it for the next six months."

"I made you an offer of a better place to stay."

"Oh, sure. With a dog and five kittens, two rabbits and a guinea pig?"

His jaw tightened. He glared.

Neely shrugged. "I'm staying, Mr. Savas. And if you don't like it, that's tough."

CHAPTER THREE

"THAT," Neely said when Frank opened the door to Cath's apartment the next morning, "was low."

She had been fuming all night, pacing and prowling. But only in her room, because Sebastian Savas had taken over. He'd come down from his shower, all clean and pressed looking and set up his computer on the desk by the window.

"My desk?" he'd asked with one raised brow.

"Your desk," Neely had replied through her teeth.

And so he'd set to work in the living room. And she'd gone upstairs to fume because she certainly had no intention of betraying how upset she was to her new landlord.

She had no qualms about telling Frank exactly how she felt, though. "Really low. Sneaky, in fact," she said now.

The look on Frank's face said that he would have shut the door on her and bolted it fast if he thought he could get away with it.

He couldn't. She'd have ripped it off its hinges to tell him her opinion of what he'd done.

"Um, hi, Neely. I, er…good morning." He peered at her from behind the door as if it were a shield. As far as Neely was concerned, he needed one.

"Good, Frank?" She raised a brow. "Not exactly." And determinedly she strode straight past the door, backing him into the living room and flinging the door shut behind her.

"Just a minute. Hang on now—" Frank was backpedaling and glancing behind him, as if to see if the window was open and might provide an escape route, no matter that they were on the third floor.

"Don't even think it," Neely warned. "If I want you to go out the window, I'll push you."

Frank almost managed a grin at that—as if she were kidding. "Aw, come on, Neel', you know I wouldn't have done it if the loan hadn't fallen through."

Neely did know it, but it didn't make her any happier. She gritted her teeth.

Frank shrugged helplessly. "I know you're mad. I'm sorry. But I couldn't help it. It just…happened."

"You didn't tell me! You could at least have told me!"

"About Savas?" He looked appalled, as if doing that was more than his life was worth.

Neely shook her head. "About my financing falling through! I shouldn't have had to find it out from Sebastian Savas walking through my front door and telling me he'd bought my houseboat! Your dear friend Greg should have told me."

Frank cursed under his breath. Then he raked his fingers through his hair. "He tried to. Honest to God," he insisted. "He didn't call me until late. Said he couldn't get hold of you. He tried your cell phone. And he didn't want to leave it as a message. So when he couldn't get you, he called me. Thought you might be at the office. But—" Frank spread his hands "—you weren't."

No. She hadn't been.

Because she'd gone sailing with Max.

He'd called her the night before and said he was thinking of buying a sailboat, that he wanted to take it out on Friday, would she come along.

She'd been stunned—and torn. "Friday? It's a workday."

"Take it off."

"But—what would my boss say?" she'd asked him, only half-joking.

Max laughed. "Guess." But then the laughter died, and he said gravely, "He'd say you were doing him a favor, getting him out. Making up for lost time."

And there had been a ragged edge to his voice that spoke of a depth of feeling that she couldn't ignore. And as it was exactly the sort of "carpe diem" philosophy she'd preached at him more than once, how could she argue?

Still she hadn't given in at once. "You're sure?" she'd pressed him.

"Well, I'm going," he'd said firmly. "Whether you come or not—that's up to you. I'd like you to," he'd added. "The question is, can you spare the time?"

Which meant he was still Max. The leopard hadn't changed his spots entirely. He might not be Max Grosvenor, the 100-proof workaholic that he'd been when she'd first walked into his office seven months ago, but there was still a lot of the old Max Grosvenor inside him. And that was good, not bad.

He just needed balance in his life. By asking her if she had time, at least it showed he was learning how to weigh choices instead of always opting for work.

"I can spare a part of the day," Neely decided. "But I need to be back by three."

"Deal," Max had said.

So she'd met him at the boatyard at nine—and she had been sailing on the Sound with Max while her financing was falling through yesterday afternoon.

She swallowed and accepted it. "Right." she said to Frank now, squaring her shoulders. "My fault."

Frank patted her on the arm. "I'm sorry," he said again. "Really. And, um, I just…didn't know how to tell you about Savas."

This last he added quickly, stepping away from her as he did so, as if he were afraid she might do him bodily harm. "Sit down," he said, pacing the floor of the apartment, but jerking his head at a chair where he expected her to sit. But Neely shook her head and remained standing.

Frank shrugged. "Suit yourself." He took a breath, raked a hand through his hair, then turned to face her. "Savas was…a gift from the gods."

"Sebastian Savas?" Neely gaped at him. Greek gods bearing gifts, perhaps? Horrible thought. "I don't *think* so."

"You know what I mean. I was tearing my hair out in my office, telling Danny what had happened, and Savas came by— working late as usual—and Danny, joking, said, hey you want to buy a houseboat. And—" Frank shrugged, still looking dazed "—he did."

Neely felt just as dazed as Frank. She'd lain awake half the night denying it to herself, convincing herself it was a bad dream. But it was actually just very bad reality, because when she'd come downstairs she'd still found half a dozen boxes of gear and a computer in the living room this morning.

"So…what happened?" Frank ventured after Neely stood there in silence, remembering the sinking feeling she'd experienced.

"Before or after Harm knocked him over the railing into the lake?"

Frank's eyes bugged. "You're joking."

"I wouldn't be capable of making that up." The memory of it still made her smile, though very little else did. "He handled it with great aplomb," she added grimly. "Just as you would expect. Swam back to the boat, pulled himself on board, stood there dripping and acted like that sort of thing happened every day of the week."

Frank was shaking his head. "And…?" he prompted.

"And then he went upstairs, took a shower, changed his clothes, ordered a pizza, set up his computer and got to work. He was still working when I went up to bed."

"He actually…moved in?" Frank sounded as if he couldn't quite fathom it. "Without any warning?"

"He moved in," Neely said wearily. There were no other words for it.

"So…what about you?"

"What about me?"

"Well, you can't…I mean surely you're not…"

"I have a lease," Neely reminded him.

"But you'll be living with Sebastian Savas!" Frank sounded as if he doubted her sanity.

"Well, what did you think was going to happen?" she demanded, exasperated by his astonished look, by the sight of his mouth opening and closing like a fish.

"I thought—" Frank shook his head "—I guess I don't know what I thought. That maybe he wanted it as an investment?" It was more a hopeful question than a statement of fact.

"He'd have been far more careful if he were buying it for an investment. This was obviously a spur-of-the-moment decision."

"I guess," Frank scratched his head. "But why?"

"Maybe he wants to make Max jealous." Neely grinned.

Frank gaped.

"I'm kidding," Neely said quickly. "But he does think I'm sleeping with the boss. And he definitely doesn't approve."

"Oh, Lord." Frank laughed at that. "You haven't told him about Max."

"Of course not. He can think what he likes," Neely said righteously. "He hates me anyway. This is just one more reason."

"Hates you?" That surprised Frank. "The Iceman?" As if he couldn't be bothered to muster up enough emotion to hate anyone.

"He thinks I design fluff," Neely qualified. Maybe that wasn't hate. But it still rankled, his haughty dismissal of her work as "girly stuff."

"He just has a different vision."

Neely gave him a wry smile. "Oh, yes. A very pointed, vertical vison."

"Be kind," Frank grinned. "You'll have to be, now that you are living with him."

That wiped the smile off her face. "Thanks to you."

"I said I was sorry. Besides, I thought he was going to find you another place."

Neely's gaze narrowed. "You discussed it with him? He knew I lived there?"

"I said I had a tenant."

"But not who?"

"Your name wouldn't sell property to Mr. Savas."

"No joke."

"So didn't he find you a place? I thought he would before he moved in."

"Oh yes, he offered me a studio."

"Well—"

"Can you see me and Harm and the kittens and the rabbits and the guinea pig and the fish in a studio? Besides," she said, "I don't want anyplace else. I want the houseboat!"

And, of course, her vehemence made Frank wince. Too bad. It was true.

She had fallen in love with Frank's houseboat the minute she'd come to see the room he had for rent. She'd been there six of the seven months she'd lived in Seattle.

When he'd said he needed to sell it, she'd instantly offered to buy it.

She loved it and, having moved so much during her youth, she'd never really felt "at home" anywhere. Not the way she had on the houseboat. To be able to buy it and put down "roots"—albeit hydroponic ones—had been a cherished dream.

"Well, maybe he'll change his mind," Frank said hopefully. "You don't know—maybe he woke up this morning and regretted it. He might be ready to move out. Then he could sell to you," he added brightly.

Neely sighed. "And maybe tonight for dinner a roast duck will fly over and fall in my lap."

Frank blinked. "What?"

"It's a metaphor for incurable optimism, Frank," she said wearily. "Never mind. Unlike you, I'm not expecting miracles. But I'll simply have to convince him to sell to me. He's all about business. I'll just have to find his price. But I am *not* leaving."

She would leave.

Sebastian was sure of it.

He'd told her pointedly last night right before she went upstairs that she had to move.

"If you don't want to go to the apartment, that's fine. It wouldn't be a good place for your animals. But you've got to go somewhere."

She hadn't answered. She'd just given him a stony stare, then scooped up all her kittens and carried them upstairs.

But she hadn't been here this morning when he got up. Granted, it was after nine and she might be anywhere. But the fact that she wasn't here boded well as far as Seb was concerned.

It was a good day. The sun was shining, and he'd had—once he fell asleep—the best night's sleep he'd had in years. There was something about being close to the water that lulled his mind, soothed his brain and sent him out like a light.

He hadn't expected that. Ordinarily he didn't sleep well except in his own bed. But last night, even despite his uncharacteristic impulse purchase of the houseboat and discovery of its unexpected tenant, once he'd hit the bed it hadn't taken long for the lap of the water against the hull, and the ever so slight movement to carry him back to his childhood, to the summers spent at his grandparents' on Long Island.

Their house was by the shore, and his grandfather had a boat that he and Seb used to take out to sail. And every now and then he would cajole his grandfather into spending the night on the boat. It had been the treat of the summer.

Last night had reawakened that long-forgotten memory. And even this morning, that was what he was thinking of as he cradled a mug of coffee in his hands and stood in front of the wide glass window that looked out across Lake Union.

Just the sight, just the memory made him smile.

Neely Robson be damned, he'd done the right thing buying Frank's houseboat. It already felt more like home than his penthouse ever had.

He went out onto the deck and had a look at Robson's painting project. The ladder was still there. She'd cleaned up the paint and brushes and they sat in a neat row on one of the built-in benches around the edge of the deck.

He studied her choice of color in the light of the morning sun. She'd painted over a gunmetal grey with a softer more silvery shade of grey. It surprised him. He'd have expected her to go for pink. Or purple. Or some other gaudy touchy-feely color.

The grey wasn't bad. It would weather well, soften in the sun and it fit in well with the surroundings. He hefted the paint can to see that there was plenty left and was pleased that there was. She'd taken down the gutters and painted them. He'd hang them back up, then take up where she left off. But first he had to go to the grocery store and buy some food.

He went back inside and plucked a piece of cold pizza out of the fridge—left over from the one he'd finally ordered last night—and ate it while he reconnoitered, getting a feel for the rest of the boat.

With Robson glaring at him—and clearly upset—he hadn't spent a lot of time looking over his new purchase.

He'd gone upstairs, then stripped off his wet clothes, showered and changed—so he had a good idea what the bathroom was like, and was grimly pleased upon looking around to discover that she hadn't overrun it the way his sisters were doing to his at that very moment.

But he hadn't wasted time upstairs. Once he was cleaned up, he came back down, opened up his laptop and set up his printer on the desk in the living room and settled down to do some work.

Begin as you mean to go on, his grandfather had always advised.

It was cliché, of course, but it was true, as well. And Seb had long ago learned the wisdom of it. It had helped him cope with the bevy of new "mothers" his father brought home. It had stood him in good stead at work.

He never tried to please. He worked hard and he always kept his own counsel. It made life simpler that way.

If people didn't like him, too bad.

Neely Robson didn't like him.

As if he cared. He didn't like her much, either.

And it would be a damn good thing when she and her menagerie were out from underfoot.

With luck, by the time he got back from grocery shopping, she'd already be packing.

Neely had never been a Boy Scout.

She did, however, believe in the motto: Be Prepared.

So she was prepared, when she let herself in the front door that afternoon, to lay a proposal on the line to Sebastian Savas.

She'd thought it all out after she'd left Frank's. Maybe he was right. Maybe by now Sebastian had buyer's remorse. Maybe he woke up this morning seasick. Well, probably not. But she could hope.

In any event, she spent three hours at the public library—because she wasn't going home—reworking her finances, then calling her mother in Wisconsin to say that things would be a little tight for a few months. Lara wouldn't care. She never thought of money anyway.

And then Neely came back to the houseboat, prepared to make Mr. Cold-Blooded Businessman an offer he wouldn't refuse.

She wasn't prepared to walk into the living room and find

herself staring out through the plate glass window at a very different man entirely.

In the seven months she'd worked for Grosvenor Design she had never seen Sebastian in anything other than a suit. Sometimes he took his coat off and she saw his long-sleeved dress shirts. And once, on a job site, she'd seen his collar unbuttoned and his tie askew. Last night, of course, she'd seen him in a suit—dripping wet.

Even after Harm had knocked him in the water and he'd showered, Sebastian had come back downstairs wearing another dress shirt and a pair of pressed dark trousers. Okay, he hadn't worn a tie. But big deal.

She'd told Max once that she thought Sebastian had been born wearing cuff links.

It didn't seem far-fetched. He wore his cool, calm demeanor like a suit of well-fitting armor. And his well-pressed, totally-together look promised the icy aloofness and consummate unapproachability which was, with Sebastian Savas, exactly what you got.

So who was the guy with the bare tanned feet and faded blue-jean-clad muscular legs braced against the upper rungs of her ladder?

Neely stopped in her tracks. But even as her body stopped dead, her gaze kept right on moving up—until it was well and truly caught by the sight of several inches of hard flat masculine abs peeking out from beneath a sun-bleached red T-shirt.

There was even an arrow of dark hair visible until it disappeared into the waistband of the jeans as the man wearing them reached up and slapped paint on the wall above the window.

Neely wet her lips. She swallowed. Hard. And swallowed again.

Her heart seemed suddenly to be doing the Mexican Hat Dance in her chest. She forced herself to take a breath—and then another—as she tried to regain her equilibrium.

It was what came of being an architect, she told herself, still combating light-headedness. They just had extraordinarily well-developed senses of appreciation for physical beauty, for strength and economy and power all wrapped up in one neat, um, package.

Perhaps not best choice of words.

On the other hand, quite possibly the most accurate, she thought as her gaze fastened on the bulge beneath the soft denim right below his waistband and framed between the rungs of the ladder.

Her face flamed and, deliberately, Neely squeezed her eyes shut tight.

She didn't see the kittens tussling right in front of her. And of course, she stepped on them.

"*Mrrrrooowwwww!*"

"Oh, help!" Neely stumbled, shrieked, caught herself against the back of the sofa and jerked open her eyes just in time to hear the paintbrush clatter to the deck and see Sebastian—who else?—skim down the ladder like a fireman on his way to a four-alarm blaze.

His gaze locked on her even as he reached down to scoop the brush up off the deck and toss it in the paint tray.

"What the hell—?"

"It's n-nothing. N-nothing," Neely said hastily.

"If it was nothing, why'd you shriek? What happened?"

"Nothing happened!" Face still burning, Neely crouched down and snagged up the kittens, clutching them to her chest and gently kneading their small squirming bodies to make sure they weren't hurt.

Sebastian jerked open the door and glowered accusingly. "Don't tell me you were shocked to see me. I live here."

That wasn't what had shocked her. She cuddled the kittens closer. "I stumbled," she said. "I landed on the kittens."

He looked skeptical, but finally he shrugged. Why did his shoulders look even broader in a T-shirt than in a dress shirt? Unfair.

"You should watch where you're going," he told her.

"Obviously." And she wasn't about to tell him why she hadn't been. Instead she buried her face in their fur and took a few more deep breaths until finally she lifted her gaze again and said, "You don't have to paint."

He rolled his shoulders. "It's my boat. Or were you going to say it's your paint?"

Neely pressed her lips together. "It is, actually. But that's not the point. The point is—" she took a breath, then plunged on "—I want to buy the boat. Still. From you."

He opened his mouth, but she cut him off. "You can't really want it. You didn't have any idea it even existed twenty-four hours ago. It's some spur-of-the-moment mad purchase for you. Maybe you think you want it now, but you won't."

He started to say something again, but Neely knew she had to get it all out now without interruption, had to make it clear how very badly she wanted the houseboat. Maybe it was foolish. Maybe it would make him even less likely to sell to her.

But yesterday, when Harm knocked him in the water and he didn't take it out on her, when he actually sounded just slightly bemused. "More harm than good," he'd said. And it was so unexpected that she couldn't believe he was totally unfeeling.

"Hear me out," she insisted. "I know you think you want it now. But you'll get sick of it. You'll hate the way the dampness makes your computer keys stick. You'll get tired of the fog. You won't want birds pooping on the deck. You'll crave your penthouse again. I'm sure you will! So, I just want you to know that, when it happens—and it will happen—I'll take it off your hands for what I agreed to pay Frank—or even ten thousand more," she added recklessly. "And I will get financing."

She'd let Max help if she had to.

She stopped and looked at Sebastian, waiting for him to say something. He didn't say a word. Half a minute ticked by. Then he said, "Are you finished now?"

"Yes." Tick, tick.

"So tell me why. Why do you want it?"

She wished he hadn't asked that. Neely loved people and

made friends easily. She'd had to, given how often she was in a new place. But she usually took her time exposing the personal side of her life. And she really didn't want to do so to a man who formed judgments faster than the speed of light.

But he hadn't said no. And he stood there now, waiting expectantly, those green eyes assessing her from beneath hooded lids.

Right. So be it. "It felt like home the first time I walked in the door," she told him. "I don't know why." And she'd given it a lot of thought, too. "We lived all over the place. Here. In California. Montana. Minnesota. Wisconsin. To say we moved around is putting it mildly. We were always somewhere different and nothing was ever permanent…not until I was twelve, anyway."

"What happened when you were twelve?"

"My mother got married."

His eyes widened, as if she'd surprised him.

"My parents weren't," she said bluntly. "My father was a workaholic and my mother was a free spirit. Chalk and cheese. Worse," she said, "they split before I was born. We stayed in Seattle for a year. But then my mother joined a commune and we went to California. Like I said, we moved around a lot. And then she met John. And something clicked. They got married. It was wonderful."

Now he really did look shocked.

"It was," she insisted. "We had a home. I loved it. For six years it was the best. Then I went away to college and—" she shrugged "—you know what college is like—nothing is ever 'home.' Then, after I graduated I lived in first one apartment and then another. Even when I came out here, at first I rented another apartment for a month. When Frank said he was looking for a roommate, I came to see the houseboat—and I felt it right away. Home. Still is." She had been looking around at everything in the room as she spoke. But when she finished she looked straight at him. "That's why."

"All emotion," he said.

She bristled. "Something wrong with that?"

He didn't answer. "Are you going to paint it pink?"

"*What?*"

It was the accusation he'd thrown at her the one time they'd worked together—that she had wanted to paint everything pink. She had ignored the accusation because it was the client who had wanted pink, and in the particular funky magazine editorial offices she was designing, the color had worked.

Now she glared at him. And he looked back impassively, one brow lifted in that sardonic way he had of making you feel two feet high.

And then his cell phone rang.

Sebastian dug in his jeans' pocket, making her aware once again of the way they fit his body, of how they gave a whole new tough rugged look to the smooth cool consummate professional she was accustomed to.

Not, she reminded herself, that he behaved any differently.

Are you going to paint it pink? What kind of a smart-ass remark was that? He'd opened her cans of paint. He knew perfectly well none of them was pink.

She scowled at him as he flicked open his phone, glanced at the phone number coming in, made a slightly wry face, then said, "Excuse me. I have to take this."

Of course he did, Neely thought. "Go right ahead," she said. But he wasn't even listening. He'd already turned toward the door.

Neely was listening, however. And she was surprised he didn't say, "Savas here," in that steely businesslike tone she always heard at work.

On the contrary, his voice was totally different with a much softer edge. And he almost seemed to have a smile on his face when he said, "Hey, what's up."

So it was a girlfriend.

She didn't know why she should be surprised. He was certainly good-looking enough. And maybe there was another side to him than the one she saw at work. Maybe he was Mr. Charm after hours. Though according to Max, Sebastian worked as many hours in the day as he did.

What he said next she didn't know because he stepped out onto the deck. Not that she wanted to eavesdrop. She had no desire at all to hear Sebastian murmur sweet nothings to his girl-friend. She couldn't quite imagine that.

But she didn't have any trouble imagining, however, the sort of cool svelte ice goddess who would appeal to him. Tall and blond and minimally curvy. Expressionless. But she might have one of those slow smiles that never quite met her eyes.

Would they, between the two of them, generate enough heat to melt the ice?

But even as she had the thought, she realized that it seemed at odds with the flicker of emotions—gentleness and calm followed by impatience and what looked like eye-rolling irritation.

And then he spoke loudly enough that Neely had no trouble hearing him at all. "Don't cry, for God's sake," he said, exasper-ated. "I hate it when you cry."

He'd made his girlfriend cry?

Whatever she said in response, of course, Neely didn't know. But whatever it was, Sebastian grimaced, sighed mightily, punched the "end" button and tossed the phone onto the hammock on the deck. Then he jammed his hands in the pockets of his jeans and glowered at it.

At least, for once, he wasn't glowering at her.

"That's not very nice," Neely said loud enough for him to hear.

He turned to look at her. "What's not?"

"Making her cry. Then hanging up on her."

"She'll call back." He came back inside, leaving the phone on the deck.

Neely frowned. What sort of submissive wimp was this girl-friend that he could treat her so badly and she'd call him again.

"How do you know?" she demanded. "I wouldn't."

"Well, you're not my sister."

Sister? He had a *sister?*

It was hard to imagine Sebastian Savas having any family at all. She'd always imagined he'd been found under an ice floe somewhere.

"I wouldn't call you back if I were your sister," she told him.

"Yeah, well, you probably aren't expecting me to pay for your wedding."

Now that did shock her. He not only had a sister, but he was supporting her?

The phone rang again. He gave Neely an arch look. "See?"

"It might not be her."

A corner of his mouth twisted. "Want to bet?"

"No. Well, aren't you going to answer it?" she demanded when he made no move to go get it.

He sighed. "Might as well. She'll keep calling until I do."

He went out again and picked up the phone. Neely stayed inside, trying to pretend disinterest.

But she wasn't entirely disinterested.

It was hard to be disinterested in a man who filled out a pair of jeans that well.

Shallow, yes. But there it was.

And it wasn't only that. There was something about this Sebastian Savas that intrigued her. Maybe it was knowing he had a family. Maybe it was watching him deal with this sister. It wasn't a short conversation they were having. And Sebastian wasn't as perfunctory and dismissive as he was at work.

I hate it when you cry, he'd said.

The Sebastian from work wouldn't have cared if the whole design team had burst into tears.

Intriguing, yes. Not that she was actually *interested,* Neely told herself firmly. Just…curious. And appreciative—in a purely academic, architectural way.

He was still annoying. He owned her houseboat. He thought she'd paint it pink. *And* he believed she was sleeping with Max!

She narrowed her gaze at him. He ended the call and tossed the phone down again, then stood there a moment, staring in her direction. But somehow Neely didn't think he was even seeing her.

What he was seeing, she didn't know.

And then her own cell phone rang.

"Hey, what're you doing?" Max asked.

She smiled. "Trying to convince Sebastian Savas to sell me Frank's houseboat."

"What?" He sounded as shocked as she had been last night when Sebastian had walked in the door.

"Long story," Neely said. She saw Seb turn to come back into the living room. "I'll tell you later."

"Tell me at dinner," Max said.

Ordinarily she would have begged off. She had gone sailing with Max yesterday. They were going out again tomorrow. Of course she was glad he was getting a life after years of having his nose to the grindstone. But his entire life shouldn't revolve around her.

"I've heard of a great sushi bar," Max tempted her just as Sebastian walked through the door and gave her a narrow suspicious look.

On the other hand, why not?

"I'd love to, Max," she said delightedly.

Sebastian's jaw tightened.

"See you at seven," she trilled and hung up. "Max and I are going out for dinner," she told him, just in case he hadn't heard.

"Lucky you." His voice was flat.

"Yes, indeed," Neely said brightly. "We've had so much fun getting to know each other."

"I'll bet." A muscle ticked at his temple.

"He's found a new sushi bar he says we have to try. I have a bit of work to do, but I couldn't say no. He made me an offer I couldn't refuse." Was she laying it on too thick?

Sebastian's expression was stony. "Did he." It wasn't a question.

"Mmm." Neely gave him one more cheerful smile. "I think I'll take Harm for a run, then come back and get ready." She grabbed Harm's leash and started toward the door. "Bye-ee."

"Robson?" Seb's voice, hard and flat turned her right around again.

"Yes?"

"You want to buy the houseboat?"

Her heart quickened. "Yes. Of course. You know I do."

Sebastian's hard mouth twisted. "Make me an offer I can't refuse."

CHAPTER FOUR

MAKE him an offer?

Like what?

Like what he supposed she was offering Max?

She wanted to strangle him. Or punch him. Or do whatever was necessary to wipe that knowing look off his handsome face.

Instead she went out with Max and grilled him about the man who owned her houseboat.

"You're interested?" Max asked. "In Seb?"

"I am not 'interested' in Sebastian Savas," Neely said, still hot under the collar from Sebastian's remark. She picked at the spider roll on her plate, poked it with her chopstick the way she'd like to poke Sebastian. "Not the way you think. He just annoys me."

"Why? Are you still ticked because he thought you wanted everything pink?" Max grinned as he regarded her over his bottle of Japanese beer.

"Not 'thought.' Thinks! He thinks I'll paint the houseboat pink!"

"Oh, I doubt that," Max said easily. "He's just giving you a hard time. Maybe he's smitten."

"Hardly." Neely sniffed. "He thinks I'm sleeping with you!"

Max's laughter was so loud and sudden that half the diners in the small restaurant turned to look at their way.

"It's not funny!" Neely fumed. She did stab her spider roll then. And her *kappa maki* for good measure.

Max shrugged and lazed back in his chair, still regarding her with amusement. "You could tell him you're not."

"I did," she muttered.

He didn't say anything, just smiled and sipped his beer.

Neely glared at him. He grinned. "He has a dirty mind," she said after a moment.

"Probably. He's a man," Max said. "And he thinks I'm in danger of succumbing to your charms."

She blinked and stared. "You knew?"

Max lifted his shoulders. "He didn't think much of me bringing you on as the living-space designer for Carmody-Blake."

"You *asked* him?"

Max shook his head. "Didn't have to. He volunteered."

Sebastian was lucky he wasn't her *kappa maki* then. She'd poked it to smithereens. "How dare he?"

"He was looking out for my welfare," Max told him. "Thinks you're out to get your claws into me."

"How dare he?"

"He understands the appeal of a pretty woman."

"He doesn't think I'm pretty. He thinks I'm weird. And he doesn't like what I do."

"Maybe he wants you."

Neely looked at Max, horrified, at the same time she remembered that odd stab of awareness she'd felt this afternoon when she'd come into the living room and spied Sebastian up on the ladder. "Don't be ridiculous," she said now.

"Just saying." Max finished his beer.

"Well, don't," Neely retorted.

She didn't want to think about Sebastian that way. And she certainly didn't want to think about him thinking about her that way!

Not that he was, of course. It was all in Max's head.

But the awareness wasn't.

She felt it again later that night. She spent the evening at Max's discussing the Blake-Carmody project. It was the work she'd have done at home anyway, but it was actually better to do it with Max. It was nearly eleven when she got home. She took Harm out for a quick walk, then went upstairs to get ready for bed at the very moment Sebastian was coming out of the bathroom. His hair was wet and he was bare-chested this time, though he was wearing his jeans, thank God.

No matter, she still felt that unwelcome sizzle of awareness. And it seemed like every time she saw him now he was wearing less. Her cheeks warmed at the thought.

He raised a brow. "Have fun?" His tone was sardonic.

"I did," Neely said, keeping hers flat.

"But you didn't spend the night." The brow went even higher.

Neely, remembering the eviscerated *kappa maki,* wished she had a chopstick on her now. She gave him a brittle smile. "It's a work night."

His expression hardened. "Nice to know you have some standards."

"Indeed I do."

He stepped past her to go into his room. The hall was narrow and he was close enough that she felt the heat emanating from his bare flesh as he passed. The sensation was almost magnetic, drawing her toward him. Quickly Neely stepped back.

He paused, one hand on the frame, as he opened the door to his bedroom. "I'm leaving for Reno as soon as Frank and I close on the houseboat at the bank."

"Rubbing it in?"

"Just telling you. I won't be back until Friday."

"Good."

A corner of his mouth tipped. "I thought you might think that." He paused. "If you need anything—"

"I'll ask Max."

His knuckles tightened on the door frame. "Of course you will. Sweet dreams, Robson." Amazing how much disparagement a man could get into so few words.

Neely ran her tongue over her lips. "Same to you, Savas."

His bedroom door shut with a hard click.

Not until it had, did Neely breathe again. Even so her knees still wobbled. And for the first time she wondered if maybe she should spend the week looking for another place to live.

So what if she was sleeping with Max Grosvenor?

What did he care?

Well, he didn't, Seb assured himself as he tossed clothes into his suitcase preparatory to tomorrow's trip to Reno. Unless it interfered with the good of the company, it made no difference at all.

All the same, he was glad he was leaving. That way he didn't have to be around to watch.

It had been bad enough before—when he'd simply caught glimpses of Neely Robson waltzing into Max's office during the day. He'd been annoyed when they left together sometimes in the evening. And, yeah, he'd felt downright irritated Friday when Max had come late to their meeting because he was out sailing with a woman half his age!

But it had been worse over the weekend. At least when he was in Reno, Seb wouldn't have to watch her chatting to Max on the phone while she fed the kittens. He wouldn't see her razor on the shelf by the shower and wonder if she'd shaved her legs before she'd gone off with Max.

And he wouldn't have to see her run out the door and down the dock to meet him when he came to pick her up.

Not that he'd been watching…

He'd been minding his own business upstairs in his bedroom, putting some books on the shelves of the built-in bookcase, when he'd just happened to hear the front door shut and had glanced out to see her dance away down the dock, waving madly at Max who was coming to meet her.

Max hadn't been exactly reluctant, either. The grin Seb saw

on his face was one of pure joy. And when she reached him, damned if he hadn't wrapped his arms around her in a fierce hug.

Boss and employee?

Yeah, right.

Just good friends?

Not even close.

Not that they were claiming any such thing. They weren't claiming anything at all.

They didn't have to, Seb thought, banging his suitcase shut.

So it was far better that he was off to Reno for the week where he could focus on what was important—his work—rather than here where he would have to watch Robson work her wiles on Max and Max be no smarter than Seb's old man.

And that was another reason to be gone. No whining from Vangie about when their father was ever going to call. And no more endless phone calls from all the rest of the pack.

As if living with Neely Robson and watching her kiss up to Max over the weekend wasn't bad enough, the Savas sisters' invasion of Seattle was driving him mad.

Now instead of simply having Vangie's phone calls to contend with, he had the triplets and Jenna, as well.

Saturday night, while Neely was out having sushi with Max, he was listening to Ariadne whine about her boyfriend she'd left back in New York. Then Alexa moaned on about the three she had left behind in Paris. And just when he'd said, "Why do you need three boyfriends?" she'd turned the phone over to Anastasia who had rattled on about her fiancé who was heading to the Trobriand Islands to do field work for six months.

He didn't even know she had a fiancé. And all he could think was, *Not another wedding.*

Maybe three boyfriends was better than one serious one. He hoped the guy stayed gone five years.

The next day—while Neely was, naturally, out sailing with Max—they'd called again. Not once. Not twice. Half a dozen times or more. To ask where the blender was. Then where the vacuum was. Then where the broom was. Didn't he have a dustpan? Did he know if the recycler would take broken glass?

"What sort of glass?" Seb had demanded. "What'd you break?"

"Oh, don't worry," one of them said airily. He never had any idea which. "Nothing important."

Probably it wasn't, he'd lied to himself. But as he couldn't make himself believe it, he'd made sure he had time, before taking them out to dinner, to drop in and survey the damage himself.

There was clutter everywhere. But it wasn't much worse than he'd imagined—and he never did figure out what had broken. It hadn't been a bad evening. The food was good, his sisters had behaved well, and he would have enjoyed himself except for periodically wondering if, while he was eating salmon, Robson and Max were feasting on each other.

It had seemed all too likely when he got back to the houseboat at ten and only Harm, the rabbit and the guinea pigs were there to greet him.

Of course, she could have come home and gone to bed. Maybe she had, he'd told himself. But after an internal debate about whether he should or not, Seb decided that, as owner of the houseboat, he was allowed to check his tenant's room. So he cracked open the door, hoping to see her soundly sleeping.

He saw an empty bed. And all the kittens escaped.

Thank God he got them all back in and the door shut. But it was after eleven and he had just been coming out of the bathroom from taking a shower when she came up the stairs.

She looked tousled and tumbled and too damn beautiful.

And his shower had not been nearly cold enough.

"Savas here."

Ah, yes. The Voice of Authority. Clipped. Precise. Pure business. And with an unfortunate slightly rough, very masculine edge that sent a frisson right down Neely's spine even though she was determined to be immune.

"Your boat is sinking."

"*What!*"

So much for clipped precise authority.

Neely smiled. Perhaps it wasn't the nicest way to convey the news that there was a leak in the underbelly of Sebastian's new property, but as it could have been *her* houseboat, she wasn't very inclined to play nice.

"You heard me," she said. "There was water all over the floor this morning."

"*Robson?*" The voice was barking in her ear now. She supposed she ought to have identified herself. "Is that you?"

"Who else could it possibly be?"

"One of my sisters," he muttered. Then "What are you talking about?"

"Water water everywhere," she said. "It means there's a leak down under somewhere. I remember it happening once before. Frank had to call someone to come and pump something out, then get down under there and fix it. Sorry, I can't get more technical than that. I can find out who he called, if you want," she added helpfully. "Or maybe you have a better idea."

There was a moment's hesitation, long enough that she wondered if he might actually have a better idea. But then he said, "Get the guy's name. Call him if you can and ask him to do it. I can't get back until Friday."

It was Wednesday evening now. He'd left on Monday, so basically she'd enjoyed a Sebastian-free week so far. It had been quite blissful.

Or it would have been if Max hadn't taken to teasing her every day, asking her if she missed him.

"Right," she said now briskly. "I'll try to track Frank down. Sorry to trouble you."

"No trouble," he said. "It's my responsibility. It's my b—"

"Your boat. Yes, I know that. Okay. Bye." She was about to hang up when he spoke again.

"Robson?"

She put the phone back against her ear. "Yes?"

"How's Harm? Pushed anyone else in the water?"

"What?" The questions surprised her. "Um, no. But there hasn't been anyone else here, either."

"Good. I thought perhaps— Never mind. How's the weather?"

"The weather?" What on earth? She was talking to Sebastian Savas about the weather? "Well, it's raining," she said. "As usual. Imagine that."

He laughed. It was a low, intimate chuckling sound that sent a quick unexpected shiver of awareness down the back of her neck.

"Not here," he said. "It's hot in Reno."

"I should think it would make a nice change." She stared out the window at the rain bucketing down and tried to imagine a bit of sunshine.

"It does. But still I'll be glad to get back."

"So Harm can push you in the water again?"

"Not exactly." But there was the unexpected sound of a smile in his voice.

Neely was having a hard time believing this conversation was happening. She hadn't wanted to ring Sebastian in the first place. She'd imagined he would be abrupt, abrasive and think she was overstepping her bounds. When he was polite about the leak, that was as much as she'd hoped for. She certainly didn't expect casual conversation.

And while it was difficult to imagine it was Sebastian on the other end of the connection, at the same time she was having no trouble seeing him—in her mind's eye—at all.

It was evening. He was on the road. She'd been there often enough that she understood the scenario. There was no noise in the background, so he wasn't out in one of Reno's nightspots. He'd likely be in his hotel room, perhaps lying on his bed.

No. Don't go there.

But even as she warned herself, a vision of the last time she'd seen Sebastian—damp-haired and bare-chested—became all too vivid, and she had to swallow hard. But before she could say a word, he spoke again.

"I don't much like being on the road," he said quietly.

And what was she supposed to do? Say, *Too bad. Goodbye?* Her mother had raised her better than that.

She said, "I don't, either. I think it comes from moving so much when I was a kid."

"Tell me about it," he asked, sounding interested.

And the invitation to talk was somehow more than she could resist. She'd been trying to work ever since she got home. But she'd been restless—not to mention periodically mopping—and now she curled up on the sofa with Harm's head in her lap and watched the rain.

"Well, I was home schooled mostly. Or should I say, commune schooled?" she corrected herself. "My mother was a hippie of sorts."

"No joke?" He sounded surprised.

"Nothing funny about it," Neely assured him. "My mother is definitely an independent free spirit. But she was never quite able to be an independent free spirit on her own. She needed a base, a group of people. But she didn't like anyone telling her what to do. Mostly communes are live and let live. But they can have their idiosyncracies, and she always seemed to run up against them. And then we'd move on."

"Just you and your mother?"

"Until I was twelve," Neely said. "And then she met my stepdad. He was a policeman. We were living in Wisconsin at the time and he'd been sent to arrest her for selling her jewelry on the street without a business license. It's funny, really," she said, thinking about those days now, "they were so different. And yet they were just right for each other. They had a great marriage. It was awful when he died. But I knew good marriages exist because of theirs. I want a marriage like that someday."

"Do you." There was a sudden hard edge in Sebastian's tone and his statement wasn't a question. "Good luck." He couldn't have sounded less encouraging.

He was such a cynic. "You don't believe in marriages that last?" She asked, at the same time wondering why they were discussing it at all. It certainly wasn't the sort of conversation she ever expected to have with Sebastian Savas. But then, she'd never expected to be living with him, either!

"I wouldn't say they can't ever happen," he said. "But I'd bet against it."

"So did my mother. And then she found the right man. You won't say that when you find the right woman."

"There isn't a right woman."

"Well, maybe not yet, but—"

"Ever."

"Oh." She mulled that over, then said cautiously, "So…is there a right man?"

There was a moment's stunned silence. Then he laughed. "No, Robson. I'm not gay. I'm just not getting married."

Firm and final. The Voice of Authority was back now. This was the Sebastian Savas she knew.

"Act like that," she said lightly, "and it won't be a problem. No one will want to marry you."

"Good."

If there was ever an exit line, Neely decided, that was it.

"Right. Well, I won't be expecting to get an invitation to your wedding anytime soon then. Thanks for warning me. I'd better go make your phone call now about the leak. And Harm wants out. Don't you, Harm?" She patted the sleeping dog who never even opened an eye. "Bye." And she rang off before Sebastian could say anything else.

Not that there was anything else to say.

But she couldn't stop thinking about the conversation, even long after she'd hung up. It was as odd as it had been unexpected. But maybe he was just bored.

Still, when her cell phone rang the next evening and she saw Sebastian's name come up on her caller ID, Neely was amazed.

"What?" she demanded, the heightened awareness she always seemed to feel around Sebastian battling with her very real desire to hang up at once.

"And a very good evening to you, too, Robson." He sounded amused, and he'd lost the clipped tone he'd used when making his pronouncement on marriage the night before. Once again she heard the slightly sexy undertone beneath his sardonic response and she wondered if he was doing it on purpose. To bait her, perhaps?

She refused to succumb to its allure. "Good evening," she said politely. "To what do I owe the honor of this call?"

"Aren't we prim and proper, Robson? Wearing pink?"

"It's none of your business what I'm wearing!" The minute the words were out of her mouth, she felt as if she'd been had. Was she always going to jump at the bait he dangled?

"What do you want?" she muttered.

She had been enjoying a quiet evening on her own and allowing herself the pretense that the houseboat was hers and hers alone, refusing to think about Sebastian Savas who had, drat his hide, invaded her dreams last night. How perverse was that?

And now here he was again.

"I want an update," he said briskly, all business. "Did the guy come and fix the leak?"

Neely breathed easier. "Yes. Took him most of the afternoon, though. He's sending you the bill. A hefty one, I imagine."

"No doubt."

He wanted to know what was done, and Neely told him as best she could. She hadn't been there the whole time. "I had work to oversee," she told him now. "I let him in, and I came back later to check how things were going. But I can't give you a play-by-play. Sorry."

"It's okay. I appreciate your bothering at all. Thanks."

"You're welcome."

She expected him to end the conversation there, but he didn't say goodbye. He didn't say anything. Still, he hadn't hung up. She could hear him breathing.

There was no noise in the background of his call tonight, either. And Neely found herself with visions of Sebastian in his hotel room, lying on the bed flickering once more into her mind. She focused on a boat zipping across the lake, trying to get rid of the visions out of her head.

"Do you know where to buy little rose-colored boxes?" he asked suddenly.

Neely blinked. "What?"

"Not for me," he said hastily. "My sister's getting married. She's been rattling on about these damn boxes she wants on the table at the reception. For mints or something. She keeps calling me and bugging me."

Neely's mind boggled. Sebastian not only had a sister, but she called him and bugged him about tiny wedding favors?

"I said, try the Internet. But she wants to see them in person," he said wearily.

Neely almost laughed at the combination of fondness and frustration in his voice. "Oh, dear."

"So, do you?" he demanded when she didn't speak.

"Why on earth would I?"

"They're rose," he said. "That's almost pink. As far as I'm concerned, it *is* pink. But Vangie insists there's a difference."

"Of course there's a difference," Neely said. "But I don't know anyplace to get them. Some wedding place, I suppose. How many does she need?"

"Two hundred and fifty or so."

"Yikes. When's the wedding?"

"Three weeks."

"And she's just now starting to look for them?"

"No. She's just now decided for sure that's what she wants. Or thinks she wants. What difference does it make? How the hell long does she have to have them anyway?"

"Not long, I suppose. But…I should think she'd want things prepared."

"Oh, she does," Sebastian said grimly. "But she keeps changing her mind. Or having it changed for her. First they were silver. Then they were rose. Then they were silver and rose. Now they're rose again. For simplicity's sake," he quoted wryly. "And God knows how many more times it will change. Since the rest of them got here, it's four times worse."

"Rest of whom?"

"My sisters. Not all of them, but more than enough."

"All?" Neely said faintly. He'd mentioned one. That had been surprising enough. And now there were more? "How many sisters do you have?"

"Six."

"*Six?*" She gaped, unable to imagine it.

"And three brothers."

"Dear God."

"At last count."

"What!"

"My old man has a habit of getting married and having kids," Sebastian said grimly. "It's what he does."

"I see." She didn't, and she suspected Sebastian knew that. The whole notion of ten kids in a family astonished her. And then there was the "my old man has a habit of getting married…" part.

Did his "old man" have a habit of getting divorced as well?

Was that what was behind Sebastian's complete cynicism toward marriage? She could understand that. But somehow, even though he'd brought it up, she couldn't see herself asking him.

Still, that alongside the nine brothers and sisters would go a long way toward explaining Sebastian's standoffishness. When you were one of ten, you probably needed to draw pretty definite boundaries. But from where she stood, as an only child, there was a definite appeal to the sound of all those siblings.

"You're so lucky," she told him.

"Lucky? I don't think so."

"I would have given anything for a sibling or two."

"A sibling or two wouldn't necessarily have been bad," he said heavily. "It's nine of them that gets old."

"I suppose." But she wasn't sure. She thought it sounded like far more fun than being dragged around from commune to commune after her mother.

"It's why I bought the houseboat," he told her. "They were moving in on me."

That was why? She sat up straight on the sofa. "All of them?"

"Four of them. Four too many." She could hear the edginess in his voice.

"Just until the wedding?"

"God, I hope so. In fact, no question. After that, they're gone." There was certainly no doubt in his mind about that.

"So, when they're gone, will you sell to me?"

He laughed. "My God, you're persistent."

"When I want something, yes. Will you?"

"Like I said, Robson. Make me an offer I can't refuse."

"And what would that be?"

"You're a smart cookie. Max is always saying so. Figure it out."

The sight of the houseboat at the end of the dock made Seb smile.

He was always happy to get home. Like he'd told Neely on Wednesday, he didn't like being on the road. He didn't mind working all hours, but at the end of the day he liked his own place, his own space. Solitude. Peace and quiet. There had always been a sense of calm when he walked through his front door.

But there had never been a sense of anticipation before.

His heart had never kicked up a notch. On the contrary, it

usually settled and slowed. But today, all day long while he was still in Reno going over the building specs with the contractors, in the back of his mind Seb was already on his way home.

Ordinarily he would have stopped and picked up some take-away for dinner. But tonight he didn't. He thought he'd wait and see if Robson was hungry. If so, they could get something together.

It wasn't a date.

It was just a courtesy. They were sharing living space for a while. So, the way he saw it, they could share a meal.

Besides, he owed her. She'd called him about the leak. She'd arranged for the repair. She had been the one who'd had to come home and let the repairman in.

So he would buy her a meal. It was the least he could do. Simple.

But when he opened the door, she wasn't there.

"Robson?"

Silence. Except for the dog. He was there, stretching and yawning and thumping his tail madly as Seb came in and dumped his suitcase on the floor and briefcase on the table.

The kittens were there, too, purring and meowing, noticeably bigger and even friskier than they had been on Monday. They attacked his briefcase and his shoelaces with equal enthusiasm. One scaled his trouser leg, putting tiny claw holes in the fine summer wool.

"Hey, there!" Seb lifted it off and cradled it in his hands. "Robson? You here?"

The guinea pig whistled. The rabbit didn't even look up from crunching on its dinner. No noticeable change in them and, thank God, no more of them, either.

And no Neely anywhere.

He felt oddly deflated. Of course he had no right to expect her to be there. They hadn't discussed dinner. It would have seemed like a date if they'd discussed it.

Well, it wasn't a date, that was certain. It wasn't anything because she wasn't here.

It was only seven, though. Maybe she'd worked late. God knew he did often enough. So he took a shower and changed clothes and came back downstairs hungrier than ever.

Still no Neely.

There was however a blinking light on the desk phone. It wasn't his phone. But he wasn't sure it was Robson's either. If someone had left a message for Frank, he'd have to pass it on. Seb punched the message light.

"Neel'." It was Max's voice. "Couldn't reach you on your mobile. Left you a message, but thought I'd try you at your place. I'm running late. Just go on in. I'll be there."

Go on in?

Go on in *where?* His brain couldn't help asking the question even though, in his gut, he already knew the answer. But before he could follow the thought any further, his own mobile phone rang.

He answered without even glancing at the ID. "Savas."

"Oh, good. You're there!" Vangie's voice trilled in his ear. "Are you home? In Seattle, I mean?"

Seb slumped on the sofa. A kitten launched itself and landed in his lap. He winced. "Yeah. Just got back."

"Great! We thought you'd like to come have dinner with us." She was all bubbly and bright and eager. Seb could hear lots more bubbly bright female voices in the background. "See the progress we've made for the wedding!" Vangie went on. "Want to?"

No, actually he didn't. Dealing with five of his sisters was very close to the last thing Seb wanted to do tonight.

But he said, "I'll be there."

Because the absolute last thing he wanted to do was sit home and think about the implications of Neely Robson having a key to Max's house.

Neely was humming "Oh, What a Beautiful Morning" when she let herself in the front door at eleven the next day.

It was beautiful—sunny and bright with not much wind. Not

enough to go sailing, she'd told Max when she left his place, which was fine because she had other things to do.

"Hey, there," she said dropping her tote bag and kneeling as she threw her arms around Harm who launched himself at her. "Did you miss me?"

"He didn't, actually," a harsh male voice said, "because he had me to take him out last night and this morning."

Neely's gaze jerked up to see Sebastian standing at the entrance to the living room. He was backlit and she couldn't really see his features, but she had no doubt he was scowling. She gave Harm one last happy cuddle and stood up warily.

After their two phone conversations during the week, she'd dared hope they had reached some sort of friendly rapport. Obviously she was wrong.

"I didn't neglect him," she said firmly. "I arranged for Cody to come in last night and early this morning.

"Because you knew you were going to spend the night?" Sebastian demanded.

"Yes."

He didn't say anything, but she could hear his teeth grinding.

"Is there a problem? I called him this morning to make sure he'd come over and he said he did. Are you saying he didn't?"

Sebastian opened his mouth, then shut it again abruptly. He shrugged irritably and shoved his hands in the pockets of his jeans. "I never saw him." He turned away and stalked into the living room.

Neely tossed her tote bag onto the stairs to carry up later, then followed him. "Were you here?"

He turned back to face her. "I didn't spend the night elsewhere, if that's what you mean?"

"Unlike me?" Neely said, capable of filling in the blank.

"Yes. Unlike you." He bit out the words. "Was it worth it?"

"Oh, yes." She gave him a bright smile. "It was great. We had dinner and then we went upstairs and—"

"Spare me the details," Sebastian snapped. "How old are you?"

Neely blinked at the sudden shift in topic. "Twenty-six. Not that it's any of your business."

"He's fifty-two!" The words burst from his lips. He wasn't scowling now; he was glaring furiously.

It took Neely a second to make the leap. Then she narrowed her gaze. "You're talking about Max, I presume?"

"Damn right, I'm talking about Max! That's not to say he isn't well preserved. For his age, I guess he could be considered a stud—"

"A stud?" Neely's jaw dropped. "*A stud?*" She stared at him for three seconds, and then a giggle escaped her. It seemed to infuriate him.

"You know what I mean! But for God's sake, you've got skills, talent. You win prizes! You don't have to sleep with the boss to get ahead!"

She hesitated only a moment. Then she twirled a long curl around her finger as if considering the question.

"Oh, I don't know," she said. "I believe it's a tried-and-true method in some companies."

Sebastian's jaw locked. She thought she could see steam coming out of his ears. Served him right, she thought.

"And as you say, Max *is* very attractive…for his age." She giggled again, as if enjoying some private reflection.

"You're more attracted to me than you are to Max." He said the words flatly, yet there was a wealth of challenge in them, and he looked at her as if daring her to deny them.

She opened her mouth, then shut it again. She arched her eyebrows at him provocatively. "You think so?"

"You know you are," he insisted. "There's been a spark between us since day one."

This time she opened her mouth and didn't shut it, still trying to formulate the words. She gave a careless, dismissive shrug. "In your dreams, Savas."

But Sebastian didn't wait. "You want proof?" He closed the space between them so that she had to tip her head up to look at him. His mouth was bare inches away. She could see the whiskered roughness of his jaw, could feel the heat of his breath.

She swallowed. She blinked. She waited.

And the next thing she knew Sebastian's lips came down on hers. Neely had certainly been kissed before. She'd known her share of masculine mouths, their hard warmth, their persuasive touch. She'd opened to them, dared to taste them in turn. And she'd always been able to keep her wits about her, to think, *hmm, kissing is interesting, but no big deal.*

All of a sudden, right now, with Sebastian Savas's mouth on hers, it became a very big deal indeed.

There was the hard warmth and the persuasion. But there was more—a hunger, a need, a seeking, a question looking for an answer.

And her mouth knew the answer even as it asked questions of its own.

It wasn't just a spark, either. Though she would have had to admit, had she been capable of rational thought, that yes, she'd sensed it, too.

This was far more than a spark. It was a fire, burning hot and fast, fanned to full flame. And the deeper the kiss, the less the fire was quenched. It raged and consumed, hungry and desperate and edging toward out of control.

His arms came around her, slid up her back, drew her closer so that their bodies leaned, touched, pressed. She had never felt like this, had never wanted a kiss to go on and on. Had never kissed without caring where her next breath came from because she knew—she was sharing his.

She lifted her hands and touched his back, his shoulders, the nape of his neck. Her fingers threaded through short crisp hair, then fell to clutch his shoulders as her need spiraled, her hunger grew.

And then, abruptly, Sebastian pulled away to stare down into her eyes, his own lambent with arousal, his breathing harsh. "Does Max kiss you like that?"

Stunned, shaken and absolutely furious—as much at herself as at him, Neely could barely find the words. "No one kisses me like that!"

Sebastian smiled a satisfied feral smile. "So dear Max isn't perfect after all? I'm not surprised. It's what you get, trying to get it on with a man old enough to be your father."

Neely's heart was still slamming in her chest as she wrapped her arms across it and hoped she didn't look as rattled as she felt. "I wasn't trying to 'get it on' with Max. We were working."

"All night?" Sebastian scoffed.

"No, but until two. And then I went to bed. Alone. In the guest room."

"Yeah, sure. So, you're saying you're just friends, is that it?" Sebastian mocked her.

And Neely slowly, firmly shook her head no. "We're not just friends." She lifted her eyes and met Sebastian's knowing look. "He's my father."

CHAPTER FIVE

"YOUR *father?*" Seb stared at her, poleaxed. His heart hammered, his body clamored, and he didn't believe a word of it. "He is not."

"He is. Max is my dad." Robson insisted, her chin jutting as if she was daring him to take a poke at it.

Seb was sorely tempted, especially after he dragged in a desperate breath and looked at that chin more closely, spying something familiar in the shape of it as he did so.

God Almighty, was she really Max's daughter? Was that the female version of Max's chin he was seeing? He stared at her, stunned, still disbelieving.

Robson glared right back, eyes flashing. And the longer and harder he stared the more Seb realized that the color of her eyes was the same stormy blue of the man he'd just accused her of sleeping with.

Oh, hell.

The boss's daughter. And he had just kissed her senseless.

Worse, it wasn't only Neely Robson who'd been senseless with desire. He'd been right there with her—wanting her.

And now…now he wanted to kill her.

Ordinarily Seb went to ice when his emotions were frayed. He was all steely coldness when he needed to be. But his emotions were beyond frayed at the moment. And he went beyond ice and straight into meltdown.

"What the hell were you playing at?" he demanded.

"*Me?*" She arched her eyebrows in a way that annoyed him. As if she had nothing to reproach herself with.

"Never mind." He cut her off before she could speak. "I know damn well what you were doing! You were baiting me, trying to get me to make a complete ass of myself!"

"You did that all by yourself," she informed him airily. "And I did not bait you."

"The hell you didn't! 'Max is very attractive...for his age'!" He flung her words back at her in a mocking tone. "That's not baiting?"

"I was agreeing with what you said. You're the one who called him a 'stud' first. You're the one who accused me of having an affair with him! You've been accusing me practically since the day you met me!"

"And you've been acting like he was your long-lost lover!"

"Or my long-lost father."

She said the words quietly, but Seb was too incensed to care. "You didn't have to lead me on. You could have said, 'He's my father,' anytime at all."

"I could have," Neely agreed. "But why should I?"

"Because it's the truth!" he shouted.

At the fury of his explosion, Harm put back his head and howled.

"Now see what you've done!" Neely dropped to the floor and wrapped her arms around the dog, shushing him. He stopped howling and happily licked her chin.

"I didn't do anything," Seb said gruffly. "He was just yelling at you, too."

"Was not." Neely's voice was muffled against the dog's fur. She hugged him tightly.

Seb scowled down at her, still infuriated. "Stop hiding behind that dog."

At the accusation her head jerked up, and she threw him a dag-gerlike glare. But when Seb just stood there staring at her implacably, she scrambled to her feet, threw her shoulders back. "I am not hiding behind anything—not my dog, nor my father. And I did tell you—just now."

"Thanks a lot," he said sarcastically. "Thoughtful of you. Got any more…revelations, Robson?" He arched a brow at her. "Is your mother the Queen of England maybe?"

"Who's baiting whom now? And my mother is exactly who I said she was."

"A hippie who just happened to have a fling with the most uptight workaholic in the western hemisphere?"

"She had a relationship with Max. They lived together."

Seb's eyes widened in surprise.

"They did," Neely insisted. "They were young," she said. "And in love."

"Sure they were."

"See?" Robson pretended to pout. Aiming those moist, luscious lips at him. "There you go again, making judgments, jumping to conclusions! That's exactly why I didn't say I was Max's daughter in the first place. If I had, you would automatically have assumed that he'd given me the job because he's my father."

"And he didn't?" Seb asked sceptically.

"No, he didn't. He didn't give me my job at all. He's not even the one who hired me. Gloria Westerman in personnel hired me."

"You never met with Max?"

She folded her arms across her chest now and leaned back against the bar between the kitchen area and the living room. "I never met with Max."

"But you knew he was your father." It wasn't a question.

Robson nodded. "Yes, I knew. But he didn't know who I was at all. I hadn't seen him in years. We moved to California when I was four."

"And you never saw him again?"

"Not until November when I came to work. And then I didn't want him to know who I was. I use my stepfather's last name.

Max didn't know it. I wanted to make it on my own before I told him."

Seb rubbed a hand against the taut cords at the back of his neck. He was still ticked by her having gulled him with her pretense, but he could appreciate the reason she had given for not telling Max or anyone else who she was. If he was honest, he knew that in her shoes, he'd have been tempted to do the same.

"You're not telling me he still doesn't know, are you?" Because there was no way on earth he'd believe that.

"No, of course not. After I won the Balthus Grant and he invited me to work on the Wortman project with him, I knew I had to. If we were going to be working together, I wanted him to know. Besides by then I'd won the grant, so I knew and he knew—and so did everyone else—that I could do the job. See?"

Seb grunted. He rocked back on his heels, muttering under his breath. Yeah, he saw. It made sense, what she'd said. But it still annoyed him.

"You could have told me."

"Like you told me you were buying the houseboat!"

"That's not the same thing at all!"

"No? Well, it sure felt like it. One minute I thought I knew what was going on—I was buying a houseboat from Frank—and the next minute you walked in and it was yours! My home belonged to you!" "

Her face flushed again, the heightened color making her more beautiful than ever, and Seb felt an overwhelming urge to stop arguing and kiss her again.

He took one step toward her and she said abruptly, "Stay away!"

He stopped, brows drawing down. "Stay away?"

"Yes." She wrapped her arms even more tightly across her breasts as if she were cloaking herself in body armor.

He gave her a sardonic look. "You're going to go all cool and detached and claim that I forced myself on you? Another pre-varication, Robson?"

Her lips pressed in a tight line. "I'm not lying, Savas. And I'm not claiming any such thing. But—" and here she shook her head fiercely "—you're not doing it again."

"Why not? You liked it. You kissed me back."

Let her deny that if she dared.

For a moment he thought she might, but then she shrugged. "Yes, I did."

"So…why stop? Don't you like kissing? It felt as if you liked kissing," he told her with a knowing grin.

"Kissing's fine." Her voice rose, as if she were going to say more, but in the end, she didn't. She simply shook her head.

"But…?" Seb coaxed her.

Her eyes flashed. "But there's no point!"

He could definitely think of a point to a passion as hot as the one that had raged between them. "Seems like we could have come up with one." He grinned again.

Robson didn't. "Well, one point," she allowed. "I suppose we could tear each other's clothes off and make—have mad passionate sex. But we're not going to."

"You don't like sex?" He'd noticed how she cut herself off, changed what she'd been going to say. Make love.

"It's fine," she muttered.

"Ah, kissing's fine. Sex is fine, but…" he goaded her now. "But what, Robson? You're frigid? Can't convince me of that." His body was still humming from the heat generated by their passion.

"I'm not trying to convince you," she fired back. "I'm just saying it isn't happening again. Not with you."

Their gazes met, locked, battled. Dear God, he wanted to stop fighting with her and take her to bed!

"You wanted me," he argued.

"I already admitted to that. I'll say it if you want—my body wants yours." She flung the words at him. "But I don't do 'sex for sex's sake,' Savas. I don't do 'one-night stands.'"

"No one said anything about one night."

"I don't do 'affairs,' damn it."

"You're a virgin?"

The flush on her face deepened. "No. I'm not a virgin. But I've learned my lesson. And I want sex to matter. I want it to mean more than just making my body and yours feel good. I want it to be an expression of love, commitment, even marriage!"

He gaped at her. "*With me?*"

"Good God, no! With the man I fall in love with!"

Seb opened his mouth to argue—and shut it again.

The smile Neely gave him was both bitter and knowing. "Exactly," she said.

It could have been worse.

Neely told herself that over and over, like a mantra, as she huddled shivering in a perfectly warm shower. Right now it didn't seem like such a beautiful morning after all.

It wasn't telling him about Max that bothered her. That bit of information was long overdue and she knew it. She hadn't known how to work it into the conversation. Somehow "Oh, by the way, Max is my dad" just wouldn't fall easily from her lips.

Still didn't.

But he knew it now. And that was pretty much the least of her problems.

She could have been swept away by his damned kiss.

She could have slid her hands under the soft cotton of his T-shirt to caress the hard-muscled warmth of his back. Could have lain right down with him on the sofa and lost all her inhibitions.

Could have, let's be honest, done exactly what she'd said when she'd thrown the "we could tear our clothes off and have mad passionate sex" words at him.

No, not *could* have. *Might* have.

Or even more accurately, *would* have, had Sebastian not stopped when he had.

Neely was beyond mortification. It didn't bear thinking about.

And yet, she had to think about it—to come to terms with it.

You never got past things you didn't face. She'd learned that from all the years she'd spent watching her mother simply move on rather than confront her demons.

But after having come within a hair's breadth of making mad passionate lo—having mad passionate sex—with Sebastian Savas, God help her, a little retreat and regroup seemed in order.

So she had taken her tote bag and what was left of her shattered composure and climbed the stairs.

There she took a shower, washed her hair, scrubbed her body and, especially, her face, as if she could remove every vestige of Sebastian's kiss, and tried to get a grip on her life.

She should move out.

But if she did, he'd think she was running away from him.

"You *are* running away from him, idiot," she said aloud, wringing out a cold washcloth and pressing it to her face, tried to reduce the heat she still felt.

But even so, she resisted actually running. She wasn't a wimp. She was a strong intelligent capable woman.

"Reduced to putty by a single kiss." She said that aloud, too.

But she knew, even as she said the words that it wasn't being reduced to putty that bothered her. Perversely the feeling was one that she'd often hoped for.

It was the way her mother had said kissing John made her feel. It was also the way she'd felt with Max.

In all honesty, Neely had longed for that feeling. Had begun to wonder if she ever would. And now she had.

With Sebastian Savas!

Of all the unsuitable men—a man who didn't do love, who didn't do commitment, who didn't do marriage.

Not that she wanted any of those things with him. God forbid.

But why did she have to feel that way, *need* that way?

And why in heaven's name did it have to happen now? With him?

A part of her wished she hadn't admitted who her father was.

If she hadn't, she could have thrown herself into the charade of being Max's girl.

But even as she thought it, Neely remembered telling Sebastian that she wasn't hiding behind Max.

And she wasn't, damn it!

Still, she would have liked to spend the rest of the day—or the rest of her life—in her room. But that was just another hiding place. So she dried her hair and got dressed and went back downstairs, not sure what to say now. Not sure what to do.

Only sure she wasn't kissing Sebastian again.

No question about that.

He was sitting at his computer working with his CAD program as she entered the living room. He had his back to her, but she saw him stiffen at the sound of her footsteps. Harm padded over and nudged her hopefully, then ran to the door.

"Yes," she said, relieved for the suggestion. "We'll go for a run." But she had something to say to Sebastian first.

She waited impatiently until he finished whatever he was doing, then she cleared her throat. For a moment she didn't think he was even going to bother to turn around, but finally he spun his chair around her way.

"It's not going to happen again," she said.

He blinked. "What's not?"

Oh, great, he was going to pretend it hadn't happened?

"The kiss," Neely said. "Any kisses." She felt like an idiot saying it, expecting he would shrug and say, "Nobody asked you," but he didn't.

He scowled. "Because you think I'm coming on to you because you're the boss's daughter?"

That hadn't even occurred to her. But before she could say so, he went on fiercely. "Well, forget it. I don't do that sort of thing ever."

"Oh." She paused. "Um, good." Pause. "I guess."

He looked at her, apoplectic. "You guess?"

"Well, I wasn't thinking you were. I mean, you didn't know, did you? When you…kissed me?"

"No, I didn't know! Then. But now I do and—" his tone was measured, but his gaze was not. It was simmering and intense "—I just want it to be clear."

She nodded. "It's clear. But really, it doesn't matter."

He blinked, then looked quizzical.

"Because it isn't happening again. No kissing," she repeated.

"Why?"

Now it was her turn to be apoplectic. "I told you why! Because kissing has to lead to something!"

"It does."

"To love? To marriage?"

"To bed," he said. "What's wrong with that? Or do you never kiss without wanting a proposal first?"

"What I don't do is kiss without any kind of possibility of commitment!"

"Ever?" He sounded stunned.

"Well, I just did, obviously." And the truth was, she wasn't that stingy with her kisses when they didn't matter. It was when they did—when they threatened to make her lose all sense of propriety, when they could have her tumbling straight into bed without a thought for tomorrow or next month or next year—yes, then she was very stingy indeed. "No kisses," she said again and met his disbelieving gaze with unblinking ferocity.

"You are a dinosaur," he told her.

"I am a dinosaur," she agreed. Better he think that than think she was a complete pushover.

He stared at her, then shook his head. "You just expect us to live together completely platonically when we could burn the boat to the ground with a kiss?"

"Yes."

He barked a laugh, but it wasn't a joyful sound. "Sure you don't want to move out, Robson?"

"I'm sure," she lied. She thought perhaps she ought to be

running away as fast as she could. "We are, after all, adults," she reminded him.

"I'd say that's the problem, not the solution."

"We have self-control," she went on relentlessly. "Or I do," she added. "Don't you?"

His teeth came together. "I have self-control, Robson," he said flatly, just as she had hoped he would.

"So it won't be a problem, then. It will just be hands off," she said brightly.

For a long moment Sebastian didn't say anything. Then he agreed gruffly. "Hands off."

"And…mouths off?"

"What are you, a lawyer?"

"Just covering…all eventualities. So, no kissing?"

A muscle ticked in his temple. "I already said that."

"Just making sure." But at the same time she was extracting the promise, she was staring at him sprawled there in that chair. He was still wearing a pair of running shorts and a T-shirt that treated her to far too much visual stimulation. Sebastian Savas with his long bare legs splayed and his muscular arms flexing as he cracked his knuckles did disastrous and very unfair things to her libido.

It wasn't fair that such an unsuitable man should be able to make her heart kick over and her pulse quicken and other intimate parts of her body tingle with the mere awareness of him.

Their gazes met. And held. And held some more.

Sebastian swallowed. And even the sight of his Adam's apple moving in his throat was an enticement.

The discovery made Neely gulp. She moistened her lips with her tongue.

Sebastian shut his eyes. "Oh, for God's sake, just get the hell out of here."

There.

It was simple.

Mind over matter. Or libido. Or something.

It wasn't as if she wanted to want Sebastian Savas, after all. He was the last man she should be interested in.

She wasn't interested in him.

Much.

It would have been easy—or at least *easier*—if he'd had to go back to Reno. But he didn't. He was there—on the houseboat whenever she got up in the morning, coming out of his bedroom just as she was getting out of the bathroom. Coming abruptly face to breastbone with his bare chest was not conducive to pure innocent thoughts.

And then he would come downstairs looking all polished and professional—long-sleeved pale-blue starched dress shirts and dark trousers that should have looked like body armor but on Sebastian looked sexy as hell because she had no trouble imagining the hard-muscled man beneath them.

He was there at work, too. Not often. They didn't work together. She was working with Max on Blake-Carmody, and Sebastian was doing whatever it was Sebastian was doing—but every now and then she caught a glimpse of him, caught him looking at her.

And abruptly they would both look away.

And no matter what she was doing or saying or supposed to be doing or saying, in fact she was thinking instead about what it had been like to kiss him.

It wasn't just one day or two. It was the whole week. Day in, day out.

"What's the matter with you?" Max asked. "You don't have your eye on the ball."

No, she didn't.

She had it on Sebastian Savas.

It was the stupidest thing he'd ever heard.

No kissing!

What was she, a department store dummy? No feelings? No urges? No needs?

Of course he could control his libido—but why should he? It wasn't as if he was going to get emotionally involved.

Was she?

The thought brought him up short. He wasn't used to dealing with women who wanted more from him than he was inclined to give.

Did Robson want more? Was she in danger of falling in love with him? Was *that* what she was saying?

Of course she wasn't! She hated his guts for saying she designed doll houses. She was attracted, that's all.

And resisting.

So she'd come up with a silly rule.

Well, fine. He could abide by it. It wasn't as if he spent every day thinking about Neely Robson…imagining her lips under his…fantasizing about kissing her.

Well, he hadn't until the day he'd actually done it.

And now, damn it, he couldn't seem to forget.

It would have been easier if he'd got to go back to Reno this week. But no, he was stuck in Seattle the whole time, running into her first thing in the morning when she was still sleep-rumpled and soft-lipped.

"Oops, sorry!" she said, and skittered out of his way. But not before she'd brushed against him doing so. And how the hell was he supposed to just pretend his body didn't leap in response to that?

And then he came downstairs to find her playing with the kittens or sitting in her rocking chair cuddling the rabbit under her chin or nuzzling the blasted guinea pig—and his fingers itched to take the animal out of her hands and pull her into his arms and do a little nuzzling and cuddling of his own.

Ordinarily he got away from her at work, but it was uncanny the number of times he ran smack into her in the hallway and she licked her lips, startled, and he couldn't help staring straight at them.

Almost worse was going into the blueprint room to see her

leaning over the drafting table, her derriere so neatly outlined in her navy trousers as she'd sketched something in for Max. At the sight he'd slopped his coffee on his hand, making him curse.

Worst of all, though, was seeing her disappear into Max's office and knowing perfectly well that she wasn't in there coming on to Max at all.

She was perfectly free.

And—by her own decree—totally off-limits. Sebastian ground his teeth at the pointlessness of it.

But then he reminded himself that sex was simply a biological urge. Any appealing woman would do.

Only his father seemed to feel the need to marry them.

Sebastian didn't. Sebastian wouldn't. So he either had to put her out of his mind and find someone else to occupy his wayward thoughts. Or he needed to change her mind.

Soon.

The best defense might be a good offense in football and war and all those sweaty fierce masculine pursuits.

But as far as Neely could tell, the best defense for dealing with the effect Sebastian Savas was having on her was going out, keeping busy—and meeting other men.

"Running scared?" Max said when she told him she was playing intramural volleyball on Monday nights and going bowling on Wednesdays after work. She had gone to book discussion group at the library on Tuesday and she was giving serious thought to taking Harm to obedience class on Thursdays.

Any dog who knocked people into the water needed obedience, didn't he?

"Running scared?" Neely echoed Max's words and tried to invest them with as much scorn as possible. "Of what, pray tell?"

"Your roommate," Max said. He arched a speculative brow and regarded Neely with amusement.

She was beginning to wish she hadn't bothered to stop in his office on her way to the gym. "Why would you say that?" She couldn't be that obvious, could she?

"You never felt the need to get out every night when you were living with Frank." Max shrugged. "And you didn't last week when Seb was in Reno."

Neely glared at him. "Don't you have anything better to do than work out my motivations?"

A grin flashed across Max's face. "You're my daughter. I'm catching up on all the years I never got to be a father."

"If you want to practice all the things you missed, Mom's coming out this weekend."

Abruptly Max's smile vanished and he straightened up in his desk chair, put both feet on the floor and gave Neely a hard look. "Your mother and I are past history."

Neely gave an airy wave of her hand. "Just thought you'd like to know."

Max grunted. "Go bowl."

She did. She even went out for a beer with the group afterward. It was nearly nine when she got home. Sebastian was working at the computer. He didn't turn around when she came in, but kept working while she made a fuss over the kittens, then scratched Harm's ears and said, "Hang on. Let me put my stuff upstairs and I'll take you for a run."

"I already did."

She blinked as Sebastian spun his chair around and met her surprise with an unsmiling stare. "Oh. Well, um, thanks."

"And I fed the cats and the rabbits and the guinea pig. Maybe you shouldn't have animals if you're not going to take care of them, Robson."

Neely straightened, eye wide. "I beg your pardon? Who says I don't take care of them?"

"Well, you're gone all day and all night—"

"I came home at lunch and took Harm for a run. I came home before I went bowling and fed him and took him out. I fed the kittens. I played with them. I took the rabbits out on the deck. I *never* neglect my animals! And if you think I do, then you can—"

Sebastian raised his hands, palms out. "So, fine, you do take care of them, I didn't know. You weren't here. At least you're not here whenever I've been here. Which must take quite a lot of effort on your part." He paused and then repeated, "You aren't here. I wonder why…." He let his voice trail off.

Their gazes met and she knew Sebastian knew exactly why she wasn't here.

She waited for him to suggest, as Max had, that she was running scared, but he just said gruffly, "Anyway, I took him for a run."

"Thank you." Her tone was stiff. And she turned away to clip Harm's leash on his collar anyway.

"I'm leaving in the morning," he said to her back. "Back to Reno. So I won't be here to walk your dog. "

"I'm sure we'll manage," she said, still not looking at him, heading toward the door.

"Or kiss you senseless."

She spun around and stared at him.

He smiled. "Only saying."

It was far better that Sebastian was gone.

Really, it was. She didn't have to keep bumping into him in the hallway or on the stairs. There was no T-shirt hanging on the hook in the bathroom tempting her to pluck it off and breathe in the subtle scent of him. There was also no coffee container sitting on the countertop because he'd forgotten to put it away, and no running shoes by the door to trip over, and no pair of smoky-green eyes watching her every time she looked up.

It was a relief all the way around.

So why did the place seem so empty?

It wasn't empty, of course. Harm was here. The kittens were here. And the rabbits and the guinea pig.

It was exactly the way it would have been after Frank left.

Exactly the way it was when Seb had gone to Reno after the very first weekend he'd bought the houseboat. It hadn't been lonely then, had it?

Well, actually, now that you mentioned it…

No! Forget it. And it was true that she did breathe easier while he was gone—though she still felt his presence everywhere.

But she had to admit she was surprised and a little disconcerted when Friday came and Sebastian didn't.

She didn't go out on Friday night, actually sat home and worked and played with the kittens and, heaven help her, played the violin that Sebastian had brought with him.

Why not? She thought crossly. *He* never played it.

She was always careful to put it back where she found it. She didn't think he ever knew she'd touched it.

She shouldn't touch it. And yet she couldn't seem to keep her hands off.

She'd missed not playing, but she hadn't realized how much until she began again. It had nothing at all to do with it being Sebastian's violin.

Nothing!

Saturday her mother arrived and there was barely time to think about Sebastian, except to be grateful he wasn't there. Her mother wasn't going to stay with her; she'd arranged to stay with a friend on Vashon Island. But of course Neely was picking her up at the airport and would take her back to see the houseboat.

Still she hoped he hadn't come back while she was at the airport. She didn't think Sebastian needed to meet her mother, and she was quite sure Lara didn't need to meet Sebastian.

She hadn't seen her mother since going back to Wisconsin at Christmas, but Lara was the same as ever, rather like the weather—mostly sunny and with scattered clouds and the occasional rain shower whenever she teared up remembering "the good old days" with John.

"It's so empty without him," she told Neely in the car on their way from the airport to Lake Union. "Even after all this time."

"I know," Neely agreed, because it was—and because knocking around the houseboat the past two days had given her a glimmer of how empty life could seem—and how aware she was of a man who wasn't there.

"But he'd be glad I'm out visiting you instead of staying home," Lara went on as they drove north from the airport. "I can hardly wait to see your houseboat."

"Oh, er, about the houseboat…" Neely hadn't told her mother about what happened. Now she did, and watched Lara's consternation grow.

"You're sharing a houseboat with a man?"

"I've always been sharing a houseboat with a man. This is just a different man."

"What sort of man?"

"He's like Dad. A workaholic architect. Totally consumed by his job." Well, almost.

Lara looked appalled. "Like your father? You're not sleeping with him!"

"*What?*" Neely almost drove into the side of a fish seller's van.

"Of course you're not. You're far more sensible than I ever was." Lara shook her head at the memory. "But if he's really like your father you have to be careful."

Tell me something I don't know, Neely thought. "I am being careful, Mom," she said with more assurance than she felt. "You don't need to worry. We have an understanding."

Lara muffled a snort. "You might. Does he?" she asked sceptically.

"Of course he does."

"Mmm." Lara's doubts were evident. "If he's like your father he can be very persuasive."

"Mom!"

"I'm only saying," Lara said defensively. "Max was very determined."

Thank you for sharing, Neely thought, reasonably certain she could have done without the knowledge. "Speaking of whom, are you planning on seeing him while you're here?"

"Not likely," Lara said. "He wasn't pleased that I took you and scarpered."

Neely blinked. "You did?"

Lara made a noise that might have been agreement. "He was very bossy. And he expected me to just fall in with whatever he thought we should do. Or not do. And then, he worked all the time and I was just supposed to get the leftovers—a few minutes here and there, which there were damn few of," she said darkly. "He didn't even have time to get married." She shrugged. "So I left."

"Really?" The details had never been forthcoming before. It must have been coming back to Seattle that coaxed them out of her mother.

"Yes, really. What was I supposed to do? Just sit around and wait for him to come to his senses? Hardly likely. Max wasn't the type. So I thought I'd do something dramatic, like leave. And he'd wake up." She laughed a little bitterly. "The more fool I. He hated all that commune stuff so when I took off for the place near Berkeley, I was sure he'd come and grab us both back. But—" she shrugged "—he didn't. So it's good I left. He had a lousy sense of priorities."

Neely had been barely four at the time they'd decamped for the commune. She had few memories of her father from those days. Mostly she remembered waiting and waiting for him to come and pick her up—and then her mother saying, "I guess something really important happened. Let's you and I go to the park."

Now she gave her mother credit for not bad-mouthing her father when she easily could have.

"I think he might have changed a little," she said now. "He does go sailing with me."

"Hasn't stood you up?" Lara said with a wry look.

Neely shook her head. "I bet if we invited him to dinner, he'd even come." Though in truth she wasn't sure at all.

Lara just shook her head. "Don't play matchmaker. Your father and I had our chance. I came out here to see you and to get together with Serena." That was the friend she was staying with. "I've had a good marriage. I have no intention of trying to rekindle a fire that burned out a long time ago."

"You don't even want to see him while you're out here?"

Lara shook her head. "Only if he were tied down so I could tell him a thing or two without him running off to a meeting."

And given her father's less than enthusiastic response to the news of her mother's visit, Neely didn't think that was likely to happen. She kept her eyes on the road. But as she took the off ramp for Lake Union, she thought there was something almost ironic in discovering that her mother might be able to teach her something about dealing with men after all.

CHAPTER SIX

"IS SHE gone?"

The voice on the phone was Max's. It was midmorning on Sunday and Neely had just come back from taking Harm to the dog park to run with his buddies for an hour.

"From my place or from the state?" Neely replied, not having to ask who he was talking about.

"The state."

"Nope. Not for a couple of weeks. But she's not here if that's what you're worried about."

"I'm not worried," Max said gruffly. "Thought I'd drop off the specs for Blake-Carmody, but not if she was there. Want to go sailing after?"

"I can't. I'm meeting with Stephen Blake tomorrow morning. I need to get all the designs in order. Mom's out on Vashon staying with a friend. Why don't you take her sailing?"

"Don't make me laugh."

When Max showed up an hour later he still wasn't laughing. In fact he was edgy and kept glancing around, as if he expected a jack-in-the-box to pop out of a cupboard, rather like she was whenever Sebastian was around.

Only it was more amusing to witness someone else's agitation rather than feel her own.

"Why isn't she staying with you?" Max asked without preamble. Again Neely didn't have to ask who.

"Who would she sleep with? Sebastian?"

Max, who had been prowling the living room, jerked and spun to stare at her.

"Kidding," Neely said lightly.

Max's face cleared and he managed a grin. "Very funny." He gave himself a little shake. "Sure you don't want to come?" he nodded in the direction of the harbor where his new sailboat was moored.

Neely shook her head and picked up the portfolio she was working on. "Duty calls."

"Carry on, then," Max said, and left as quickly as he'd come.

In the silence he left behind, for the first time Neely actually did get some work done. Heaven knew there was plenty to do, and she'd been distracted all week. Now she didn't sit around waiting for the other shoe to drop—or Sebastian to walk in the front door.

So she was deep in a sketch of one of the condos' living spaces when the sound of the doorbell jolted her and sent her pencil skittering across the pad.

"Drat," she muttered under her breath, but got up to answer it, nudging Harm out of the way so he didn't launch himself enthusiastically at the kid selling cookie dough or magazine subscriptions or at Cody's mother, come to ask if she could borrow a cup of sugar.

Mentally she prepared to say no to the cookie dough and magazines and yes to the sugar, provided they had any. But when she opened the door there was a young woman standing there looking as surprised to see her as Neely was.

She was probably close to Neely's age, maybe a bit younger, certainly curvier, which her shorts and halter top all too clearly revealed. She was tall and tanned and had the most gorgeous honey-and-sunlight-colored windblown mass of hair Neely had ever seen.

They stared at each other in silence.

Then Harm, whom Neely held by the collar, said, "Woooof!" in his big deep bloodhound voice, and the other woman's gaze jerked down to see him and her eyes got even wider.

"I must have the wrong houseboat," she said, rapidly starting to back away. "I'm looking for Sebastian Savas. But I've obviously got it wrong. Excuse me. I—"

It took Neely this long to get her own tongue untangled. "No," she said, "you don't. This is…I mean, he lives here."

And obviously had enough time for at least one gorgeous woman.

"He does?" The woman's voice almost squeaked. "With you? I mean…I didn't know he…well, heavens."

Which was not quite what Neely was thinking, but close.

"He's not here now though," she went on, telling herself she was very glad to have met Sebastian's girlfriend. She could stop thinking about him at all now. Could stop wishing…

"Oh." The other woman managed a sort of smile.

"I don't know when he'll be back," Neely said. "He's out of town. But I can tell him you came by."

"Er, I'm not sure you should," the woman said. "He'll probably go ballistic."

As opposed to being The Iceman? Neely thought. Though it was quite some time since she'd considered him icy in the least. Rather she thought he smouldered. And that was conceivably worse.

"He didn't tell me where he lived," the woman confided. "And now I know why." This time she took her time as her gaze swept over Neely appraisingly.

Oh, dear. "I'm not—I mean, we're not—I think you're misunderstanding," she said quickly, not wanting Sebastian's girlfriend to get the wrong idea. The last thing she wanted was Sebastian blaming her for the bust-up of whatever sort of relationship he had with this woman. "He's not my boyfriend," she assured the woman. "You don't have to worry."

The woman laughed. It was a real laugh, too. "I think you're misunderstanding, too. He's not my boyfriend, either. He's my brother."

Neely goggled. "Your—"

"Brother. Well, half brother, really. The best one in the world," she said firmly. "For all that he's a little, um, secretive, at times. He never mentioned *you*. Do you…live with him?"

"Yes, but—"

"That sod! He's living with a woman? After he told me *NEVER* to live with Garrett before we got married—"

"Oh, you're the bride?" Neely felt oddly as if a weight had been lifted from her shoulders.

Sebastian's sister nodded. "I'm Evangeline. Everybody calls me Vangie. Who are you?"

"Neely Robson. I work with your brother."

Vangie looked as if she was sure that wasn't all Neely did with her brother. But she didn't argue. She just knelt and put her arms around Harm. "And you two even have a dog! We never had pets."

"Er, well, Harm is mine, really," Neely said.

"But you share him," Vangie decided. "Seb always wanted a dog. But my mother didn't want to be bothered. And then Matt's mother didn't. Or the triplets' or—"

"What?" Neely stared at her.

Vangie shrugged. "I'm glad he has a dog now," she said simply. "He's finally getting what he deserves."

Neely wasn't sure at all about that. But then again, she wasn't sure what Sebastian Savas deserved.

His sister, however, gave Harm a fierce hug and looked up at Neely with her luminous green eyes suddenly awash with tears. "I just hope I do," she said, and the tears started rolling down her cheeks.

Good grief. Not given to drop-of-the-hat emotional displays herself, Neely stared, nonplussed for several seconds before she said, "Are you all right?" which was a stupid question because who burst into tears if she was?

Vangie gulped and blinking rapidly stood up again. "I'm f-fine. I just…wanted to talk to Seb. He gets me through everything. Always has. And I know he wouldn't expect me to show up here, but I thought he would understand…and help and…" She broke off and wiped her eyes on the back of her hand.

"Do you want to come in?" Neely asked because somehow she didn't feel she could just shut the door on Sebastian's sister, especially when she was crying.

Vangie gulped, then brightened visibly. "Would it…be okay? I mean, you don't know me. But you do know Seb," she added a bit more cheerfully. "You live with Seb, and—"

"Not the way you're using the term," Neely said again.

But Vangie had apparently decided that, yes, she did want to come in because she stepped past Neely into the hallway, then followed a tail-wagging Harm into the living area beyond.

"Ohhh," she exclaimed, looking around avidly. "I love it! It's so much nicer than Seb's penthouse."

"It is?" Neely blinked.

"Well, you know what I mean—friendlier, homier." Her eyes went straight to the guinea pig and the rabbits. Then one of the kittens who was on the back of the sofa launched himself at her and she gave a little shriek as she caught him in her hands.

Her gaze turned to meet Neely's, "It's a miracle."

"What's a miracle?"

"You…them—" she waved the kitten around as if encompassing the whole room "—this. And Seb. Unbelievable."

"The dog isn't his. Neither are the kittens. Or anything else—except the computer," Neely said stiffly.

"I'm sooo happy for you. And him."

Obviously his sister didn't listen any better than Sebastian did. For the moment Neely gave up.

"Can I get you some iced tea? A soda?"

"Iced tea would be lovely." She had better manners than her brother at least.

While Neely poured two glasses, she watched as Vangie explored, as politely as possible—definitely not like her brother—the downstairs living area. She ran appreciative fingers along the tops of the waist-high bookcases, studied the books on the bookshelves, all the while cuddling the kitten who'd leaped at her. Then scooping up another one, she went to kneel on the window seat and look out at the deck and the lake beyond.

"Here we are, then," Neely said, coming up behind her and holding out the glass.

"Oh, thank you." Vangie turned, blinking, and Neely could see more tear tracks on her face.

"Oh, dear," Neely said involuntarily. "You're not all right."

Vangie blinked rapidly and set down a kitten to take the glass. "I am," she said, managing a watery smile. "It's just…I don't know what to do! Seb always tells me and—"

"I can believe that."

Vangie looked startled. "Oh, I don't mean he's bossy," she said quickly.

"I do," Neely muttered, but then she smiled. "I'm sure he's not so bossy to you."

"Not often. He's so kind. And he listens!"

"Does he?" How unusual, Neely thought. Obviously there were bits to Sebastian that she had missed. Or that he had never allowed her to see.

"He's the only one who's been here for me through all the wedding preparations."

"Ah, yes. He mentioned your wedding." And the little colored boxes. But Neely didn't bring that up.

Vangie nodded and sipped her tea. "I know it's been hard for him, me calling him up at all hours, bothering him at work. It's not like he cares about any of it," she confided, which Neely found both astute and surprising.

"But he cares about me. He cares about all of us," Vangie went on. "And I know, if anyone can make Daddy come to my wedding, it's Sebastian!"

Her green eyes were wide and bright, an equal combination of eager and desperate.

"Are you sure?" Neely asked cautiously. Because while she didn't know much about Sebastian and his father, the one thing she did know was that, on Sebastian's side at least, there seemed to be no love lost at all. She didn't get the feeling he had much to do with his father.

Vangie bobbed her head. "Oh, yes. And he has to! Garrett's family think it's all a bit strange that Daddy hasn't turned up yet. And I keep saying he's a very busy man, that he'll be here for the wedding. But—" she gulped "—I don't know if he will!"

"Why don't *you* ask him?"

"He doesn't answer his phone. He doesn't answer e-mails. I don't even know if he gets them. He's in Hong Kong or Timbuktu or someplace like that. That's what I told Garrett. But well, it's a little odd—if you don't know Daddy. And Garrett's parents are—" the tears threatened again and Neely offered her a tissue "—wondering what sort of family he's marrying into."

"He's not marrying them," Neely said firmly. "He's marrying you."

"But they're asking!" Vangie wiped her eyes, then strangled the tissue. "And Garrett would like to meet him, too! He never has. And…and it's not *normal* to have a father who doesn't even show up at your wedding! For once in my life—just once—on my wedding day I'd like to be normal." Vangie said fiercely. "You understand, don't you?"

Actually, Neely did. All those years in the commune had made her long for a normal family life. It had mattered a lot to her when she didn't have a father to speak of. And the one she'd had once her mother married John was every bit what she'd thought it would be. And hadn't she come out to Seattle to try to establish a relationship with Max?

So who was she to say Vangie was wrong. She gave Sebastian's sister a gentle smile and patted her hand. "I understand."

Vangie swallowed and managed a smile. "I knew you would. You'll ask him for me, won't you?"

"What?" Neely started. "Me? Ask your father to come to your wedding?"

"No," Vangie gave a strangled laugh. "Not Daddy. Sebastian! To ask Daddy." She was nodding her head eagerly now.

"Don't be silly," Neely said. "Your brother doesn't listen to me."

"Of course he does," Vangie said. "He lives with you."

"Not the way you think."

"He cares about you."

Now it was Neely's turn to blink. "What?"

"Well, he must or he would have thrown you out. And he let you keep all your animals and—"

"It's a free country and I have a lease."

"That wouldn't matter to Sebastian," Vangie said confidently.

"He won't listen," Neely insisted.

Vangie set down her glass and reached out to grasp Neely's hands in hers, imploring her, "Try. Please just say you'll try."

"It won't help. It might hurt." *He doesn't like me,* she wanted to say. But she couldn't say that with confidence anymore. Truth be told, she didn't know how Sebastian felt about her. Only that he liked kissing her—and if she weren't careful he would do it again.

But saying that would not convince Vangie that Neely had no influence on her brother. Wordlessly she shook her head.

But Vangie didn't let go. She just clung to Neely's hands. "Please."

"I'll tell him you came by." Neely relented at last. "I'll tell him what you wanted. I can't promise any more than that."

Vangie looked at her with her heart in her eyes. Then, she pressed her lips together and her eyes shut. She squeezed Neely's hands between hers, and Neely got the worrisome sense that there was some praying going on and she was somehow involved in it.

Then Vangie opened her eyes again and smiled a beatific smile. "Thank you! You're a dear!" And she lunged forward to give Neely a fierce hug. Then almost before Neely could get a breath, Sebastian's sister bounced off the window seat, bent to give Harm a hug, too, then started for the door.

It opened just seconds before she reached it.

"Seb!" And she launched herself into his unsuspecting arms.

"What the—!" Sebastian dropped his suitcase and caught his sister with what were clearly the reflexes of long practice, hugging her to him with an obvious fierce affection at the same time glaring over her head at Neely.

"What's she doing here?" he demanded as if she had orchestrated the whole thing.

"You're asking *me?*"

He eased Vangie away from him to look down into her eyes. "What's going on?" he said, and Neely was once more caught by the mixture of love and exasperation in his voice.

"I need you to talk to Daddy," Vangie said plaintively. "Please!"

Sebastian's face hardened. He opened his mouth, but then his gaze went to Neely and grimly he shut it again.

"I think I'll just take Harm for a run," she said briskly, grabbing the leash. "You two have things to discuss."

"Oh, but you can stay and—" Vangie began.

But Neely was already brushing past them. "Lovely to meet you," she said to Sebastian's sister and, giving both Vangie and Sebastian a bright smile, she chivvied Harm out the door.

He was back.

Right when she least expected him, of course.

And maybe she was "running scared" as Max had accused her, because the very sight of him in the doorway sent her heart kicking over double time. And seeing him with his sister didn't help.

It was far easier to think of Sebastian as a coldhearted, cold-blooded iceman. And far harder to resist him when she knew how very hot-blooded he was—and how warmhearted his sister, at least, considered him.

"Which does not make him a good man to get involved with," she reminded herself more than once as she and Harm walked mile after mile, determined to stay away as long as possible. He was kind to his sister, yes. He was—though he might deny it— a family man.

But he didn't want a relationship. He was adamant about that.

And Neely didn't want anything less.

"Remember that," she said out loud, making Harm look back at her quizzically as if it were a command he didn't quite understand.

It was. But not for him.

She felt relieved, then, to open the front door and find the houseboat completely quiet. The only light was the one above the stove that she could see down the hall. Sebastian must have left again. Probably with his sister.

Despite the tears, Neely was sure that the two of them would have come to an agreement. And she had no doubt that Vangie had convinced him to contact their father.

Neely unclipped Harm's leash and shrugged out of her windbreaker, then padded out to the darkened living area. It was one big room, really, just carved into a living room space over by the deck, an office space, where she stood now, and a kitchen, where she should go feed her grumbling stomach.

But she wasn't hungry—or not for food. Her soul seemed restless still for something more sustaining. And so, almost automatically, she clambered up onto the cabinet where she could reach onto the top shelf of the bookcase. She'd done it so often now that she could take the violin and bow down in the dark.

The truth was, she'd played it a lot this week. The music soothed her restlessness, calmed her and focused her. And if Sebastian was going to come back tonight, she'd need to be calm and focused.

She resined the bow, tuned the violin and began to play.

She played her Mozart etudes and her Bach minuets. Harm never started to howl until she got to the Vivaldi. And she told herself he wasn't really protesting, he was moved and was singing along.

She could see him silhouetted against the lights from Queen Anne Hill that shone across the water, his head lifted as he warbled while she played, when all of a sudden a voice said, "Cut that out!"

The bow screeched across the strings and stopped abruptly. Harm's accompaniment lasted a couple of seconds longer.

Then another silhouette rose, this one from the far side of the sofa where he'd obviously been lying in the shadows. And Sebastian turned her way and said, "Not you. The dog."

Horrified, Neely stared at him, her fingers strangling the bow. They suddenly felt so clammy she was afraid she might drop it or, worse, the violin. "I thought you were gone!"

"Think again." Sebastian came around the sofa and crossed the room toward her. Neely set the violin down on the cabinet top as carefully as she could and backed toward the kitchen. A stupid move, if she'd thought about it, as there was only one way out.

"I'm sorry," she said quickly.

"Why?"

"I shouldn't have played it. I—"

"It was meant to be played. That's what it's for." He was much closer now. Practically looming over her, and there was nowhere to go.

"Yes, but you don't play it," she protested.

"Because I can't," he said simply.

"What?" She stared at him, astonished.

He shrugged. "I never learned. It's my grandfather's violin. He played it. Almost as well as you," he added after a moment, a corner of his mouth tipping up, his tone reflective.

Neely swallowed, still wary, but beginning to realize he wasn't angry. "Thank you. But I still…should have asked."

"When? You were never here when I was." He was sort of smiling now, teasing a little.

She didn't want to be teased, didn't want to smile back. Wanted to hang on to her sanity. Definitely needed to resist.

But Sebastian said, "You can play it whenever you want. However much you want. You're very good."

"Not very," Neely said. "You have low standards."

He shook his head. "I don't, you know." He was quite firm about it. And he was barely a foot from her now, definitely looming. Also smiling.

Neely, feeling the force of the smile, sensing the electricity that always seemed in danger of sizzling between them, felt herself melting. She raised her palms, then discovered that the only place to put them was on his shirtfront.

Quickly she let them fall to her sides again, cleared her throat, tried to look for a way to duck around him.

"If you think you ought to give me some recompense, though, I'd understand," Sebastian went on, his voice almost a soft purr.

"You mean pay for the privilege? I could do that," Neely said. "It's a terrific violin. I've never played one that good. How much do you want?"

"How about a kiss?"

She jerked back so hard she hit her elbow against the countertop edge behind her and winced. "Ow!"

"Or I could kiss it and make it better," Sebastian said, reaching for her arm and lifting it, then pressing his lips to her elbow before she even had time to think.

The tingle of the touch of his mouth against her skin sent a shiver all the way up her arm and her spine to the back of her neck.

"For heaven's sake!" she protested, trying—and failing—to tug her arm away.

But Seb hung on, bending his head over it, giving her more

tiny kisses, making her tremble as he worked his way up her arm to her shoulder, her neck, her ear, her jaw.

She made a helpless noise somewhere in the back of her throat—telling herself that she didn't want this. But every part of her, body and mind was telling her she wanted it very very much indeed. She just didn't want to pay the price. The price of having her heart broken.

Her body sank back against the line of cupboards below the countertop. And instinctively she braced her other elbow on it while trying to keep her knees from buckling from the effect he was having on her.

The kisses nibbled their way along her jawline as soft strands of his hair brushed against her cheeks, her lips. She breathed in the scent of him—woodsy shampoo with a hint of the sea mixing with something simply Sebastian. If she lived to be a hundred, Neely knew she would never forget it.

And then his lips reached her chin, touched her mouth. His tongue teased its way over her lips, parting them, tasting them—tasting her.

She sighed, reached for him. Clung. And kissed him back, because she was powerless not to. She kept remembering Vangie's desperation, her words of praise for her brother, her steadfast belief that no matter what the problem, Sebastian would make it right.

And she saw how much he cared for his family.

If he were, through and through, the blackguard she'd first imagined, if he were as icy and indifferent as he'd tried to be, she thought she might have been able to hold out.

But she couldn't. He even let her play his grandfather's violin.

She opened her lips to his and hung on and, for the moment at least, let herself enjoy the ride.

One thing Sebastian Savas was extremely good at, one thing at which he positively excelled, was kissing.

Neely couldn't imagine why she'd ever thought he was cold.

Certainly there was nothing cold in the feel of his mouth on hers, nothing icy in the touch of his hands as they slid around her waist and lifted her onto the countertop so he could step up between her knees. And there was absolutely nothing frigid about the way he made her feel.

It was a long kiss, a hungry desperate kiss, and it wreaked havoc with all her earlier determination to resist him.

He wasn't good for her. He didn't want what she wanted. But even knowing it, she couldn't seem to pull away. She could only hang on and savor what was happening between them.

It wasn't until his fingers slid up beneath her shirt and began to work on the clasp to her bra that she realized more was happening than the simply wonderful drugging taste of him. And she was torn, battling with herself first before she pulled her arms away from his back and pressed them against his shoulders.

"No," she said raggedly. "Don't. I don't want this."

His fingers stilled for a moment. He drew back enough to look down into her face, his own taut with desire.

"You do," he said, and his gaze dropped to watch the rise and fall of her breasts, then lifted to look at her lips before he met her eyes again. "You want me. Don't lie, Neely."

She swallowed and nodded jerkily. "All right, yes. I want it. But not what will come after. I don't want what you want!"

"What's that?"

"Sex."

"You don't want sex?" He looked incredulous.

Of course she wanted sex, wanted to make love with him. But his words said it all. Not making love—sex.

"You know what I mean! We already discussed this. It's why I said no kissing. No one-night stands!"

"I think I can guarantee it will be more than one night," Seb said with smile.

But Neely's eyes flashed fire. "Stop it. Stop willfully misunderstanding me. I want love. Maybe that sounds hokey to you.

But it's the way I think, the way I feel, the way I want to live my life. I don't want just sex. I want a future. I want a relationship that will last." To love and be loved.

"You know any of those?" Sebastian's tone was bitter. But he stepped back a bit, put some space between them. His breathing was still ragged. "Max some sort of poster boy for long-term relationships, is he?"

"No, of course not. But my mother and John were. Or they would have been if John hadn't died. What they had was deep and real and lasting."

"You don't know their relationship would've lasted."

"I do. I know it. Here." And she put her hand over her heart in a gesture that she supposed was corny to him, but it shut him up.

He grimaced, jaw tight, then shook his head and heaved a sigh. "You're going to be a pain in the ass about this, aren't you? You're really serious."

Neely nodded gravely. "I'm really serious." She managed a faint smile, thinking how hard it was to be sensible when she really wanted to finish what they'd started.

At least Sebastian had stepped back far enough that they weren't touching now. She pulled her knees together, sat up straighter on the countertop. "Why were you lying there in the dark?"

There was still barely enough lights from the moonlight and the lights on Queen Anne Hill for her to see his expression now that he'd moved away. He'd been staring out into the darkness, but now he looked back at her sharply. "What do you mean?"

"Just what I said. You don't usually do that. You're usually working."

"I've been working. I worked all weekend, damn it. I got home looking forward to a little respite and damned if Vangie wasn't here! No respite in that."

"She thinks the sun rises and sets on you."

He raked his fingers through his hair. "She's wrong."

"Obviously she knows she can depend on you."

"For sensible things she can. Not for this." And abruptly he turned and walked out of the kitchen.

Surprised, Neely jumped down off the counter and followed him. "You're not going to do it?"

"Hell, no! If she wants the old man at her wedding, she can invite him."

"I gather she tried."

"Exactly. And he ignored her. Just the way he'll ignore me."

"She didn't think so."

"She thinks what she wants to think!" He was pacing around the living room now, cracking his knuckles.

And Neely, watching, could feel the agitation rolling off him in waves. "Is she the first to get married?" she asked him. "Of all of your brothers and sisters, I mean?"

"Yes. But what difference does that make?"

"I don't know. I don't know him."

Sebastian snorted. "None of us knows him. He isn't around enough."

"I just thought, maybe he doesn't know how to be a father. Maybe he feels awkward and—"

"He ought to feel awkward!"

"But maybe if you invited him—" she put the emphasis on *you* "—as opposed to Vangie, who is emotionally involved, you could tell him how much it means to her."

"Like he'd listen," Sebastian scoffed.

Neely shrugged. "You don't know. He might. Even if he never did before, he might have changed. Max has changed," she reminded him.

"Max is not my father!"

"No. But he wasn't much good as mine, either, for a lot of years. Part of it was his fault. Part of it was my mother's. But I'm not sorry I got in touch with him again as an adult. I'm not sorry I tried."

Sebastian glowered at her across the darkened room. But it was true, what she'd said. She had been nervous when she'd applied to work for Max's firm. She'd been worried about meeting him again, apprehensive about who exactly this man was who had fathered her.

Maybe if she hadn't had such a wonderful stepfather in John she would have lacked the courage to try to become a part of Max's life. Because of John, she knew what a good father was like. Because of John, she knew a father's love.

She didn't need those things from Max. It hadn't mattered if he'd loved and accepted her or not because John already had.

That he did was her good fortune. And his, which she was sure he knew. But she didn't know anything about Sebastian's father.

Maybe it wasn't fair to suggest that he try again. Still, people didn't have to continue doing the same stupid things they'd always done.

"Maybe he's changed," Neely repeated quietly. "Only saying. Up to you."

And Sebastian's voice was flat when he replied, "Yes, it is."

CHAPTER SEVEN

HE WASN'T going to do it.

And Neely Robson had no right to act as if he was betraying his sister and his family and the rest of the free world just because he wouldn't.

His father wasn't Max. Never would be. And there was no point in tackling Philip Savas on this topic. If he wanted to come, he would. If he didn't…that was pretty much par for the course, in Seb's estimation.

But he couldn't stop thinking about it.

No, that wasn't true.

What he couldn't stop thinking about was Neely.

He'd been lying there on the sofa in the dark, thinking even darker thoughts about his miserable father and his needy sister and his whole wearisome demanding dysfunctional family, when he'd heard the door open and Neely and Harm had come in.

It was too late to get up and turn on a light and act like he was working, and the bleakness of his thoughts had made him uninclined to make an effort to sit up and act polite if she came into the room.

Besides, if she found him lying on the sofa in the dark she'd wonder what the hell was wrong with him. And he had no desire to discuss any of it.

So he'd stayed there, still and quiet, and hoped she would go straight upstairs.

Of course she hadn't. And if she'd turned on a light, he'd have feigned waking from a nap. He was tired enough.

But instead she'd got down his grandfather's violin and begun to play it. When he'd first heard her clambering up on the cabinet, he hadn't known what on earth she was doing. And the first squeaks and tunings were so unexpected that they'd startled him, making him lift his head enough so he could peer over the back of the sofa.

She was busy adjusting the pegs, tuning the strings and didn't see him at all. He opened his mouth to ask what she thought she was doing. But then she drew the bow across the strings and it became absolutely clear.

Stunned, bemused—and for the moment completely incapable of saying anything—he sank back onto the cushions.

And listened to her play.

It was a revelation. Of all the things he thought he knew about Neely Robson—even the things he'd been wrong about—he'd never once guessed she could play the violin. It hadn't entered his mind.

But the moment she touched the bow to the strings, music filled the room. Sound echoed and reverberated. Light and bright and airy, rhythmic, almost mathematical sounds. Spritely dancing sounds that made him think of spring and splashing in puddles. And then slower, broader, more soulful tones that wrapped him in a warmth that carried him back to his grandparents' home, that made him think of winter days in the house on Long Island wrapped in a blanket and sitting next to a fireplace, waiting for his grandfather to come home.

Nothing in his life had felt like that, nothing had reminded him of home—not since his grandparents had died.

She played sounds that made his throat ache, made his eyes fill, made his heart feel too large for his chest. She made him remember in a way he hadn't remembered for years all his childhood hopes and dreams and a future full of promise.

And heaven help him, he wanted it again.

No. Not just it. Not just a home, damn it.

He wanted a home with her.

He wasn't going to do it.

Neely had known it at once from the stubborn set of his jaw, the uncompromising tone, the fact that he had turned and walked out of the room right after he'd spoken.

She didn't chase after him. Didn't follow him up the stairs and into his bedroom.

Bearding Sebastian in his bedroom would not have been wise.

Going anywhere near a bed with Sebastian would have undermined all her best intentions. Her attraction to him was far too strong. She wanted him far too much.

Now she sat in her office and stared at her computer screen thinking through all the events of last night—of all the days since Sebastian had moved onto the houseboat—and she knew he was everything she wanted in a man. He was strong, caring, intelligent, honorable and sexy as hell.

But he didn't believe in love.

Not just the love of a man and a woman, but even the love of a father for his children.

Though why he should, given his experience, she could not have said.

Outside her window the rain was sheeting down and she knew she should get to work. But even though Blake had been enthusiastic over her designs this morning and had given her the go-ahead. She still felt unaccountably depressed.

It had nothing to do with work.

It had everything to do with Sebastian.

She hurt for him. She ached for him. But she couldn't change him.

So in the end she knew she had to leave him to his obduracy and his pain because she couldn't fight the one or deny the other.

The only thing she could do—and probably should do, she admitted for the first time—was find another place to live.

Her cell phone rang before she could argue with herself about it.

Just as well, she thought, punching the answer button, because there were no arguments, just the emotional tangle she couldn't get out of. And she really needed to get some work done.

"This is Neely Robson," she said doing her best business-like voice.

"Got a favor to ask." It was Max. His own voice sounded strained and a little tighter than normal.

"Name it."

"I'm at Swedish Hospital. Could you come by?"

"Sure. What's up? New project?" She thought she remembered Max mentioning something about a hospital addition bid at the last group meeting.

"Something like that." His tone was dry. "A load of pipe fell on me. I've got a broken leg."

She'd never been to Swedish Hospital. Well, truth told, she'd been born there. But she hadn't been back since.

So finding where she was supposed to go, especially feeling rattled, was tricky. And even once she'd arrived, she still had to find the emergency area and Max who had told her he was going to need surgery.

"Not till I get there!" she'd said at the end of his phone call.

"Well, I'll tell them to wait," Max said wryly. "But I don't suppose they'll pay much attention. Don't worry, kid. I'll still be here whenever you get here. I'm not going anywhere," he added wearily. "Damn it."

Neely had said the same two words several times over by the time she finally found herself in the emergency section at Swedish Hospital and hurried toward the reception area.

"I'm here to see Max Grosvenor," she said breathlessly. "I'm his daughter."

The receptionist smiled, consulted her list and said, "Yes, we've sent him to the Orthopedic Institute for surgery. If you'll just go out there and across the street." She pointed in the direction Neely should go. It was the direction she'd just come from.

Neely thanked her and hurried back the way she'd come. The multistory Orthopedic Institute was almost brand-new and definitely state-of-the-art. The receptionist there looked up Max's name and said, "He's in surgery, dear."

"But—" But of course Max was right. It wasn't up to him, and naturally they'd need to get on it as quickly as possible.

"We have a lovely area where you can wait," she said and gave Neely directions. "The doctor will come out and talk to you when he's finished."

"Thank you." Neely gave her a quick smile and, still worrying, followed the directions to the waiting area. The last time she'd been in a hospital was when John had suffered a heart attack. Swift and, ultimately, fatal. It wasn't the same thing at all.

But it had been as unexpected as Max's accident was, and somehow even though her mind told her to relax, her body was on adrenaline overload. She walked right past the waiting area without realizing it.

"Neely."

She spun around at the sound of the voice calling her name. *"Sebastian?"* She stared in consternation at the man standing in the doorway to the waiting room. "What are you doing here?"

"Max called me."

She let out a breath. Of course he had. She might be Max's daughter, but Sebastian was his second in command. Slowly she turned and walked back to the room. There were several other people sitting and waiting for other patients. They glanced up disinterestedly as Sebastian led her to a small conversational group and gestured for her to sit down.

She sat. Sebastian sat in a chair next to her. He looked calm and composed, the way he always did. The Iceman returns, Neely thought.

But looking at him more closely, she knew she was wrong. There was tell-tale strain on his face. His jaw was clenched. As she watched, he flexed his fingers, as if he would have cracked his knuckles if he'd been willing to display any feelings at all.

"Did you get here before they took him into surgery?"

"Just." Now he did crack his knuckles.

"Is he going to be all right? How bad is it?"

"I don't know a lot. Apparently they're talking about pins and plates. He didn't sound thrilled. But he didn't know too much yet. I suppose it depends on what they find when they get in to do it."

"Yes." Neely swallowed. "He's going to be livid that he won't be able to go climbing over things, that he'll have to oversee from the office."

"Yeah, well, he's not going to."

"Not going to what? Stay in the office? He'll have to!" Trust Max to not know his own limits. She shifted in her chair and gave a despairing shake of her head.

"No, not oversee," Seb said. "He's going to be laid up too long. There will be things he can do, certainly. But not the projects he has to be on the ground for. He can stay home and work on new designs. But as far as the other stuff goes, I'm overseeing or delegating."

His words took a minute to penetrate. The significance of them took even longer.

Finally Neely cocked her head. "What other stuff?" she asked.

And Sebastian ticked off several projects that she knew Max was involved in. "I'm delegating those," he said. "But I'll keep an eye on them."

"And Blake-Carmody?" she asked, because that had been Max's baby, the one he'd brought her in to work with him on. Was she going to get to do that one?

"That one," Sebastian said, "is mine."

* * *

If Neely thought Sebastian was a workaholic before Max's accident, it was nothing to what he became afterward.

"You don't have to do everything," she said. It was like a mantra, she said it so often over the next few days, because regardless of what he'd said about delegating, he didn't seem to be delegating at all.

He was up at the crack of dawn, working hour upon hour, going between the office, all the construction sites, the design meetings and the hospital where he kept Max updated but, by his own admission, "not very updated," because Max needed to rest.

Sebastian, apparently, needed no rest at all.

Or needed it less than he needed to prove something to himself.

He was gone before she even got up in the morning, and he rarely got home in time to grab a late meal before Neely went off to bed. One night he didn't come in before she went to bed and he wasn't there when she got up, so she wondered if he'd even been home at all.

"No," he said when she asked him later that morning when she stuck her head in his office at work.

"You can't go without sleep."

"I caught a nap on the sofa." He jerked his head toward the small one in his office. She couldn't imagine how anyone over the age of ten could have caught any sort of nap on it, without becoming a pretzel in the process. Sebastian was six feet two inches of solid muscle and bone. And stubbornness.

"Not good enough," she said.

He gave her a steely look. "I didn't have time, okay? I've got to get up to speed on Blake-Carmody. I have a meeting with the committee on Friday and Max said they still had some reservations about the lobby and atrium."

"Can I help? I just had a meeting with Blake. I know how he thinks."

Seb shook his head. "No. It's fine. Thanks. This is my end of things, not yours." He gave her a quick distant smile and bent over his work again.

Dismissed, and knowing it, Neely backed out of his office. But she was still concerned. And a bit peeved at his dismissal. Did he think she was only able to appreciate her own work?

Later that day she said as much to Max.

He was still in the hospital, his leg immobilized with seven pins and a plate, which he grumbled about continually. There was no way he could come to work and take some of the pressure off Sebastian. Neely knew that, but she thought he might tell Sebastian to ease up a little.

But Max just shrugged against his pillows. "He's conscientious. Doing what needs to be done."

"He's just like you," Neely countered.

"Somebody has to be," Max rejoined with a grin.

But Neely didn't smile in return. "Do you really think so?" she challenged him. "Is it really the way you'd advise him to live? After what it did to your life?"

And mine, she didn't add aloud.

Max's grin faded and he plucked at the sheet with his fingers. "I don't know," he admitted after a long moment. "I thought so when I was his age."

"And now?"

He shrugged and raked his fingers through his hair. "I can't tell him that," he said.

"Why not?"

"It's a guy thing," he said simply.

"Oh, and that means he should just work himself into the ground?"

"Not necessarily. It means he has to get his own priorities sorted out. I can't do it for him. He has to figure it out on his own."

"Like you did," Neely said, for the first time being just a bit sarcastic with her father.

Max's mouth tipped in a wry smile. "Exactly."

And Neely supposed he was right. But Sebastian didn't seem to be doing so. He kept up the dawn-till-well-past-dark schedule as the week wore on. He did turn some projects over to second in commands. But from Neely he refused all offers of help.

Wednesday, though, he was in the middle of working on the atrium proposal when Vangie had a meltdown right in his office.

Neely had been surprised to see Sebastian's sister appear in the office, but she'd been on the phone at the time and had only glimpsed Vangie through the glass window between her private space and the main room. So there had been no chance to go out and greet her, and when she'd got off the phone and looked up again, Vangie was gone.

Of course she was sure where Vangie was, but somehow turning up in Sebastian's office to say hi seemed not the smartest idea, given his current state of mind.

It didn't matter anyway, because ten minutes later her phone rang. "You said you wanted to help," Sebastian said without preamble.

"Yes," Neely began cautiously.

"Fine. Come and get her."

He hung up before she could say a word, and for a moment Neely considered simply ignoring the summons. But she had offered to help, and she hadn't put a limit on the offer. If Vangie was what he needed help with, so be it.

She hadn't expected tears. At least they were Vangie's tears, not Sebastian's, she thought wryly when she stepped into his office. Though truth be told he looked harried and harassed enough to shed a few himself.

"What's wrong?" Neely hurried to Vangie's side, shooting Sebastian a questioning look as she did so, silently querying what he'd said to her now.

"The boxes aren't silver," he said flatly, as if that explained everything. "They're grey."

"What?"

Vangie looked up, stricken, and said, "The mint boxes for the tables…a-at the reception," she gulped, "they're supposed to be rose a-and s-silver. And the rose are r-rose. But the silver are grey!" And she started sobbing again.

"End of the world," Sebastian said to Neely, "as you can see."

Neely patted Vangie's shoulder and glared at Sebastian. Professionally he'd rejected her every offer to help, but when it came to silver boxes…

But much as she felt like leaving him to deal with his sister, she couldn't. Help was help, and she'd offered.

"Come on." She urged Vangie to her feet. "Let's go see what we can do about it."

"We can't do anything about it!" Vangie wailed. "The reception will be ruined!"

"We'll see," Neely murmured. "We'll see." And she chivvied Vangie out of the office with barely a backward glance at Sebastian. He had already refocused on the atrium design.

It took a trip to the hobby shop for some silver paint and half a dozen small paint brushes to get Vangie's tears dried up. She still looked doubtful. "Are you sure it will work?"

"Of course I'm sure," Neely said because faintheartedness never won the day. "We can take care of this right now if your sisters will help."

Vangie sniffled and nodded. "They will," she said. "And my mom and my stepmothers, too."

So she got to meet the triplets and Jenna and ten-year-old Sarah, three of Sebastian's stepmothers and get a look at his penthouse digs, as well. It was enlightening.

The penthouse had probably been austere and minimalist before being overrun by the Savas women. One look around its cluttered surfaces and clothes-strewn rooms gave Neely greater understanding about exactly why Sebastian had been so desperate to move into the houseboat. Further reflection simply reinforced the notion that he was incredibly kind to all of them.

Not many men, she didn't imagine, would have allowed their siblings and stepmothers to simply move in and take over their home. But Sebastian had. And as she showed them how to add silver highlights to the boxes—which were in fact not quite as grey as Vangie had claimed—she heard plenty of stories about how many other things he'd done for them.

He was paying Jenna's college tuition. He'd footed the bill for a year's study in Paris for one of the triplets. He was helping Cassidy, a stepmother who couldn't have been much older than he was, go back to nursing school and get her degree.

"Does your father help, too?" she asked one of the triplets.

The girl looked blank. "Who? Oh, Dad? We hardly ever see him."

"We will at the wedding," Vangie said confidently. "Sebastian's organizing it."

Neely glanced at her, surprised and wondering if Sebastian had changed his mind or if Vangie was just making assumptions. It didn't seem wise to ask.

"There, now," she said. "I think that takes care of all of them." She stood up and surveyed the sea of tiny silver-highlighted boxes on Sebastian's dining room table.

Vangie beamed, then came to throw her arms around Neely. "Thanks to you," she said. She turned to her mother and stepmothers and sisters. "Didn't I tell you she was terrific? Seb is so lucky to have you."

"He doesn't have me," Neely said.

But Vangie and all the rest of them drowned her out, telling her how happy they were that she and Sebastian were together.

Arguing didn't do any good. Sebastian would sort it out, Neely decided. He would doubtless make it clear to them that they were merely roommates.

But as she drove home after sharing a dinner of pizza and salad with so many of Sebastian's relations, she envied him the joy of them and understood why, even though they exasperated him, he would move heaven and earth for them.

He loved them.

And Neely was stunned to find herself wishing that he loved her, too, the way that she, heaven help her, had fallen in love with him.

"No," Seb said into the phone. "I can't."

Which was an understatement and then some. He paced around the confines of his office and wanted to bang his head against the wall instead of sounding calm and rational on the phone. There was no way he could just pick up and fly off to Reno for a zoning commission meeting on Friday. "Sorry. But you'll have to reschedule."

"We have rescheduled," Lymond, the chairman of the medical group whose project he'd developed, reminded him. "This is the reschedule, Seb. And they aren't going to do it again."

"Then…" *you'll have to do it without me,* Seb wanted to say. But he couldn't. He'd asked them to put it off the day after Max's accident. They said they would, and now they had, and he'd promised to accommodate…

"I'll get back to you," he promised the chairman.

"The meeting's at twelve-thirty."

Seb cursed under his breath after hanging up the phone because he knew he couldn't ask them to change it again. It would be unprofessional. But he didn't see how he could be in two places at once. That wasn't unprofessional. It was flat-out impossible.

And he couldn't ask Roger Carmody and Stephen Blake to reschedule, either. Blake might be willing, but Carmody was already apprehensive about Max's having to leave the project. He'd raised a dozen questions about the public space and atrium when Sebastian had spoken with him on the phone.

It was insane. The plans were good ones. They were his, yes, not Max's. But Max had approved them. Max would argue for them if Max were able to be there.

Maybe Max would have to go after all. That would settle Carmody's nerves, they'd all be on the same page, and everything would go on according to the plans Seb had drawn up in the first place.

That's what would have to happen, he decided. There was no other way to handle it.

"Of course there is," Max said when he stopped by the hospital that night.

"Oh?" Seb raised an eyebrow. "Have you figured out how to clone me, then?"

"Don't need to. Send Neely."

Seb blanched. "You're joking."

Both of Max's brows went up. "Why should I joke? She knows the project better than anyone. She's worked with me on it since day one."

"I worked with you on it, too," Seb reminded him. "Until you phased me out."

"Yeah, and that was my mistake, " Max admitted. "But you had Reno to do, and I wanted to work with Neely. And now I've phased you back in, as you put it. Basically it's your plan we've used, and while you know it better than anyone, Neely's worked on the project the whole time. She knows it too."

"Not as well as I do."

"Which goes without saying. But she knows Blake and Carmody."

Exactly. She could undermine the whole damn thing. "She doesn't like what I do." That was the long and short of it right there.

"She's playing for our team," Max said flatly.

Seb remembered their encounter over her pink offices and his "pointy buildings"—in her term—and shook his head. Yeah, he knew Neely much better now. Certainly he liked her personally a lot better now. And that he would happily have taken her to bed went without saying.

But that had nothing to do with working with her, being on the same page with her in terms of the project. Bed was play, this was work. This was his career, his life.

"Have you talked to her about it?" Max asked.

Seb lifted his shoulders. "Haven't had time."

"You should take time."

Seb grunted. "Yeah."

Instead, after he left Max, he called back Lymond in Reno to see how things stood.

"Expecting you Friday morning. You need a ride from the airport?"

"No," Seb said grimly. "I'll be there."

He rang Roger Carmody to discuss the atrium. If he could answer the questions now on the phone, maybe the meeting would be a mere formality.

But Roger's secretary said he was out of town until Thursday evening.

"Ask him to call me no matter what time he gets in," Seb said.

But he had been tied up in another meeting when Roger had called. So all he got was Roger's voice message afterward saying, "I don't like it. We need to rethink. I'll discuss it with you tomorrow."

But tomorrow Seb wouldn't be there.

Neely Robson would.

He got back to the houseboat before ten for the first time since Max's accident. Neely was sitting in the rocker, holding one of the kittens. She looked up and smiled at him when he came in.

It was one of those Neely smiles that undermined his resolve and made him want to throw good sense to the winds and simply carry her off to bed. Not that she would let him.

All the more reason to be short and to the point now.

"I have to be in Reno tomorrow," he said without preamble. "It's unavoidable. They've rescheduled already. I can't ask them to do it again. And the Carmody-Blake meeting will have to go on, too."

"That's all right," she said quickly. "I can handle—"

"You don't need to handle anything. Just take care of your part and I'll take care of the rest next week."

Her smile faded. "I've already taken care of my part," she said a little stiffly. "The homespace is all approved."

A reminder he didn't need. "So it is," he said, aware that his tone was now even stiffer than hers. "And I wouldn't even ask you to show up, except this is supposed to be the final rundown, and since I can't be there, Max says you're the obvious choice."

"Max said that?" There was something in her tone he couldn't quite put his finger on, but Seb knew he didn't like it. It was both doubtful and challenging.

"That's right. He thinks you should be able to hold the fort." Seb met her gaze with an equally challenging one of his own. "So I'm counting on you to hold it."

Neely's didn't waver. "Consider it held."

The meeting in Reno was, for all of Lymond's hand wringing, far more of a formality than the Carmody-Blake meeting was back in Seattle.

Seb was determinedly attentive and made sure every *i* was dotted and every *t* was crossed. But in the back of his mind, he was in Seattle, mentally overseeing the meeting with Blake and Carmody and hoping to hell Neely didn't screw everything up.

He got out of the meeting at three. His fingers itched to punch in her number on his mobile phone and see what was happening. But of course, she would be in the meeting with Carmody and Blake right then and he wouldn't get an answer.

So he went to the airport and paced until it was time for his flight, telling himself she wouldn't mess things up, inadvertently, or even worse, deliberately, making clear her own dislike of Seb's designs. He didn't think she'd do him in deliberately, but how the hell did he know?

He glanced at his watch a dozen times or more, got halfway to stabbing out her number, then tucked the phone back in his pocket and kept pacing.

Right before the plane took off, though, he called Max.

"Reno's sorted," he said when Max answered.

"Of course it is." He could tell Max was smiling.

"Just thought you'd like to know."

"Sure. I'm going home this afternoon."

"Neely picking you up?" Seb asked, grabbing the chance to legitimately introduce her name into the conversation.

"Not sure."

"Haven't you heard from her?" Seb asked, not quite able to mask the worry in his tone.

"What? Oh, sure. She may be the one to do it. Said she might be busy, though."

"Busy?"

Max laughed. "I gather she has a life."

Seb didn't find it funny. "What'd she say about the Blake-Carmody meeting?"

"It went fine."

Seb ground his teeth. "What does that mean?"

"That it went fine, I guess." Max's tone was equable enough, but it didn't invite any further questions.

"Fine," Seb muttered. "I damned well hope so."

"Chill," Max advised.

"Right." Seb let out a long breath. They were calling his flight. "See you."

He tried to tell himself Max would have let him know if Neely had screwed things up for him. He tried to tell himself she'd keep her mouth shut and let him handle it when he got home. So it wasn't a good sign to find a voice mail from Roger Carmody when he landed in Seattle.

"Smart move," Carmody said jovially, "sending Neely. She and I have everything sorted. We're all on the same page now. Talk to you on Monday. Thanks."

Seb felt sick. Shafted. Was the atrium even in the design now? It was crucial to the whole design, damn it! Had his sweeping, open spaces been carved into dinky little "people-friendly" segments. Couldn't they see how the soaring planes of the atrium spoke to the human soul?

He supposed he had only himself to blame. He should have called Carmody and put off the meeting until Monday even if it looked as if he wasn't prepared. He should have insisted Carmody and Blake have the meeting in Max's hospital room if they wouldn't wait. At least Max believed in his designs.

He should have sent Danny or Frank or somebody—anybody!—but Neely Robson to meet with Carmody and Blake. God only knew what she had agreed to.

Seb was going to have her head on a plate when he found out.

He was in a cold fury by the time he reached the houseboat.

It was getting late, the sun was setting behind Queen Anne Hill. And on it streetlights were beginning to twinkle on the other side of the lake. The wind had died down and there was only a light breeze as Seb grabbed his suitcase, banged his car door shut and stalked up the dock to the houseboat.

The porch light was on, and when he opened the door, he was immediately treated to wonderful cooking smells, light classical music and Harm bounding to meet him. He dropped his suitcase, rubbed his fingers over the dog's ears and headed straight down the hall toward the open living area.

Neely was in the kitchen. She turned when he appeared, a bright smile on her face. "You're back."

"I'm back," Seb agreed flatly. He didn't smile in return.

Her own smile faltered a little. "Didn't it go well?"

"You tell me," he said.

"No, I mean Reno. You seem upset."

"Damned right I'm upset! You screwed me over. You went into that meeting and you didn't hold the fort at all."

Neely stiffened. "Who told you that?"

"Carmody! Who else?"

"You talked to him? What did he say?"

"He called while I was flying home. Left me a voice mail—all cheery and 'everything's swell.' So he got what he wanted apparently." Seb very nearly spat the words.

"Yes," Neely said slowly. "He got what he wanted." She picked up a towel and began slowly drying her hands.

Seb slammed one fist into the other palm. "I should have known better than to send you. I should have told them they had to wait and talk to me. I should have— Damn it!" He couldn't even speak he was so furious. He wanted to slam something, hit something, kick something. The kittens took one look at him and skittered for cover.

"What is it you imagine I've done?" Neely asked, her voice very even, very calm.

"I can't imagine, can I?" Seb flared at her. "I don't know what the hell you would do! You and I don't see eye to eye—"

"You and I are working on the same project. I was representing the whole project. Not just mine. Which, as you pointed out yesterday, has already been approved." She set the towel down and came around the bar to stand by the dining room table, facing him.

It was set for two. With candles already lit. Wineglasses. There was a bottle of champagne in a bucket of ice. He stared at it, then back at her.

"What did you do?" he asked her bluntly.

"You'd sent them the designs already. I met with them and asked if they had questions. Roger had a lot of them—especially about the public space, the atrium, the vastness of it."

"It sets a tone—" Seb began.

"It sets a tone," Neely said, cutting him off. "Of openness and space, but it doesn't dwarf the people because it leads them where they need to go. It provides a greenhouse sort of feel with warmth and foliage and curving lines not straight ones. It draws people in, and at the same time it gives them a break between the hustle and bustle of urban Seattle and the office they are seeking. It provides openness and the sense of shelter at the same time. It's people friendly. It's comfortable. It makes people feel welcome."

Seb stared at her.

Neely stared back. A powerful engine thrummed as the boat cut across the lake. Seb heard his own breathing more loudly.

She looked beyond him out the window. "It's all there in your plans," she went on. "We went through the drawings one by one. He asked questions because apparently he didn't have a feel for things. He needed more explanation. So I explained what your intentions were."

Seb digested that. "*My* intentions?"

Neely shrugged indifferently. "You're the one who drew up the plans."

"Max—"

"They were your plans. Max always said they were yours."

"You don't like my designs."

"I didn't like the design we tangled over. And some of your stuff is a little too austere for me. That's true. But this—" another shrug "—I could see where you were going with this. But Roger needed it spelled out, needed convincing. So…I convinced him."

She turned away abruptly then, didn't look at him at all.

"I—" She hadn't sabotaged him after all? "You actually convinced Carmody that my designs were what the project needed?"

"That's what I went to the meeting to do." Her voice was flat, hard. "It's my job."

He didn't know what to say. It came out as a hopelessly inadequate "Thanks."

"You're welcome." The words were carved in ice. She was angry, and who could blame her? He'd been an idiot.

"I mean it," he fumbled. "I thought—"

"It's quite clear what you thought. Someday, Sebastian, you're going to have to figure out that there are people you can trust."

He'd hurt her as well. Damn, damn, damn.

She still didn't look at him. Instead she reached over to snuff out the candles.

He watched as her fingers snapped out the flames. Belatedly he realized that she'd planned something special. The table was all decorated. Flowers. Wine. Candles, now lightly smoking, the acrid scent cutting across the rich smell of food.

"What are you doing?" he said, his voice hoarse. "Don't you want to eat?"

"Not anymore."

"But what about—" He gestured to the festive table.

"That? I'd thought we'd celebrate. I thought we actually had something to celebrate." Her voice was tight and she flicked a quick glance his way before taking off her apron and tossing it on the counter. She headed down the hall where she took Harm's leash and clipped it on his collar.

Only as she opened the door did she look back his way. "Obviously, I was wrong."

CHAPTER EIGHT

SHE wouldn't cry.

She *wouldn't!*

There was no way she would shed a tear over Sebastian Bloody Savas and his accusatory bullheaded idiocy!

But it didn't stop Neely's vision blurring as she hurried up the dock away from the houseboat, Harm bounding alongside, delighted at the sudden unexpected treat. She didn't know where they were going. It was very nearly dark. She was hungry and tired and she felt as if she'd been punched in the gut.

She'd been tired when she got home, but exhilarated, too. Absolutely thrilled that Roger Carmody had come around to understanding what Sebastian had intended in his designs. He certainly hadn't bothered to spell it out.

It was there in the soaring interior space and the gently meandering curves of the walks. It was there in the few rough trees he'd sketched in. But to a man like Roger, who liked every leaf drawn on every plant, it was too hazy a concept. And there wasn't enough focus on the people.

"I don't want 'em lost," he'd said to Neely over and over. "They can't be dwarfed by the damn place or they won't want to come back."

And Neely, who thought more like Roger did, but who understood Sebastian better now, had been able to take what he'd drawn and explain. "It's not going to dwarf them," she'd said. "It's going to give them a sense of spaciousness but with plan and direction. It's going to empower them."

It had taken a while, but with patience and word pictures, she'd made Roger understand.

"I see," he'd said at last and nodded. "Yes, I see completely. Why the hell didn't he say so?" he'd demanded.

"He did," Neely said. "In his drawings."

"Took you to explain 'em, though," Roger had pointed out.

"He's very good at what he does," Neely had said absolutely truthfully. "He just figured you'd trust him to get it right."

"Well, I do. Now," Roger said. "I trust you and your interpretation."

It was nice, Neely thought bitterly, that somebody did.

Before she thought anything else though, hard footsteps came pounding up behind her. A hand reached out and grabbed her arm.

"Stop!" And she did because Sebastian hauled her up short. He was as out of breath as she was. His tie was askew and his hair looked as if he'd thrust his fingers through it.

"What?" Neely said coldly.

"I'm sorry." The words seemed dragged up from the depths of his being.

But Neely just stared at him unspeaking, frankly doubting.

Even if Sebastian was sorry, she seriously doubted that he was sorry about what he ought to be sorry about.

"Look—" he dragged in a breath "—I was wrong. I apologize. I thought—" he stopped abruptly and dropped his hand from her arm, then just stood there staring down at her as he said heavily, "Well, you know what I thought."

"Yes, I do."

He raked fingers through his hair again. "You said…before…I never imagined—"

"No," Neely replied, her voice clipped. "You wouldn't." She turned away and began to walk again. She supposed that somewhere inside she was glad he at least acknowledged his mistake. But it still hurt.

In the past few weeks she had come to understand him—maybe not totally, but at least she didn't dismiss him out of hand anymore. She didn't assume he was The Iceman, the workaholic, the impersonal distant automaton she'd originally thought he was. She understood now that he was self-contained, that he didn't give of himself easily, but that he was loyal, dependable, and that he could—and did—love.

But he still apparently didn't understand—or trust—her at all.

He caught up with her and kept pace. "Forgive me?" It really was a question. It wasn't a demand. She had to give him that.

She kept walking, but raised a shoulder. "Sure. Fine."

"Come back and have dinner with me?"

She didn't reply. She continued up the pavement, but her pace slowed. "Why?" she demanded at last, stopping in her tracks and turning to face him. "So we can pretend that you understand? That you trust me? That everything is hunky-dory?"

A corner of his mouth lifted just a little. "How about because I'm starving, you probably are, too. I'm embarrassed to have misjudged you, and I wish you'd come back so I can say again how sorry I am. So we don't miss a good meal. And so you can tell me how you convinced Roger of what I couldn't seem to make him understand?"

Neely shifted from one foot to the other. She gnawed on her bottom lip. It was a far handsomer apology than she'd ever imagined Sebastian Savas would make her. Maybe she, too, had a ways to go in learning about him.

"All right," she said, and started back toward the houseboat. "Come on."

"Have you got a minute?"

Neely looked up from her sketch book to see Vangie poking her head around the corner of the door. "Oh, hi. Sure. Come on in. How're things going?"

It was a dangerous question, to be sure, even early on the Tuesday afternoon before the wedding because the big event was now only four days away.

Sebastian had stopped calling it "the wedding that ate Seattle" and had begun calling it "the wedding that ended the world."

Judging from some of the things he'd reported over the past three days, Neely thought he wasn't exaggerating much.

Over the weekend Vangie had called him in tears half a dozen times at least.

He'd forbidden her to come by and cry in person. He was still annoyed that she'd managed to track him down in the first place.

"If you have to cry, you can cry on the phone," he'd told her Saturday morning. Neely had actually heard his end of the conversation, so she knew that much was true.

The rest he reported as it came to pass—one bridesmaid dress was too long, one was too short. One wasn't silver—"it's grey," he'd said with a flash of an exasperated grin. And the other wasn't the right shade of pink.

"Rose," Neely had corrected, because she knew all about the color scheme now.

Sebastian had mimed banging his head on the wall. "Don't worry about it," he'd advised. "No one will be looking at the bridesmaids, Vange. You're the bride. They'll all be looking at you."

It was an inspired comment as far as Neely could tell. Vangie had rung off. But she'd called back again later. And Sebastian shared the details of those conversations, too.

After the wary, tentative meal they'd shared on Friday evening, he seemed to be making an effort to communicate with her. He'd made her tell him exactly how she'd explained his designs to Roger Carmody, and he'd stared at her in amazement when she'd told him.

"He couldn't see that?" he'd demanded.

"Not everyone can read your mind," she'd told him with some asperity.

He'd grinned. "I don't need everyone to as long as you can."

It shouldn't have made her quite as happy as it had. She was asking for it, Neely warned herself. Sebastian might be making an effort, but it was only because she'd made a difference to him at work. It had nothing to do with the rest of their lives.

Except now Vangie came in and shut the door and said, "He's done it!"

Neely finished the last few strokes to the bit she was working on in her sketchbook and looked up. "Who's done it? Done what?"

"Sebastian! He's seeing Daddy."

Neely felt her breath catch in her throat. "Is he?" she asked cautiously.

Vangie plopped down into the chair opposite Neely's and nodded eagerly. "This evening."

"You're sure?"

"Of course I'm sure. He told me. Said they were going out for a drink. I always knew he would," she confided. "I know he said he wouldn't, but you can count on him. We always have," she added simply.

"That's—" Neely took a shaky breath "—wonderful." She managed a smile. It felt fake because she was too stunned to muster up a real one. But as she kept it pasted on her mouth, she processed the notion and found that the smile came more easily.

"He's doing it for you," Vangie said.

"What?" That brought Neely up short. "What on earth are you talking about? Did he say that?"

"Oh, no. Of course not. But I know you're the one who talked him into it."

"I didn't! I never said a word."

"Really?" Vangie looked astonished. "I was sure you must have."

Oh, dear. Oh dear oh dear oh dear.

Because of course Neely realized that she had said something.

That day after Vangie had first come to see Seb they had discussed it, and she had told Sebastian he shouldn't resist trying to speak with his father. He should make the effort, she'd said, because his father, like hers, might have changed.

That would have been bad enough, but she remembered now an exchange they'd had over their tense dinner last Friday night. When she'd been explaining how she'd laid things out for Roger, she'd said, "I can communicate with him. You know that. You should have trusted me."

Sebastian had said, "I do trust you." But then he'd had the grace to look guilty and say, "Well, maybe I haven't always. But I will. I will trust you, Neel'."

It was, she thought, the first time he'd actually called her anything but "Robson." It touched her heart, and yet she'd forced herself to look him straight in the eye and challenge him. "Yeah, right. Prove it."

Now her guilty face must have betrayed her because Vangie gave a little bounce in her chair and said, "I knew it! I was sure you were the reason he came through."

"What Sebastian did or didn't do was entirely his own doing," Neely insisted.

"Sure. Of course. Whatever you say," Vangie agreed, all smiles. She stood up, beaming, and when Neely stood, too, Sebastian's sister threw her arms around her. "Thank you. Thank you so much!"

"I didn't do anything," Neely protested.

Vangie just shrugged happily. "You'll come to the rehearsal dinner with Seb, won't you?"

"I—"

"Of course you will." Vangie overrode any objections before she could even make them.

Truth be told, Neely didn't want to object. She wanted to go to the wedding. And anyway, Vangie was looking very much like a steamroller en route to getting exactly what she wanted.

Besides if, when he discovered the invitation, Sebastian decreed that she shouldn't go, well, she wouldn't.

But she dared to hope he would want her there.

"Of course it's what I want," Vangie said airily. "And what the bride wants, the bride gets." Waggling her fingers in farewell, she sailed out of the office.

And Neely stood watching her, wondering if she should be worrying or rejoicing that Sebastian had, against all odds, taken her advice.

He didn't say a word about seeing his father that evening.

They had a late-afternoon meeting with Danny and Frank and the rest of the project leaders for Blake-Carmody, to make sure that everyone was on the same timetable and all the pieces were in place.

While they were all together, Sebastian told them about her meeting with Roger and Steve on Friday. He congratulated her publically for having so successfully promoted the entire design package. His smile was as warm as she'd ever seen it at work. She tried not to think about the way he looked at her when he wanted her. It wasn't the best means of keeping her mind on the job.

She acknowledged everyone's congratulations and good wishes as they were leaving the room. She hung back, thinking he might say something to her then. But Danny stopped him with a question, and she couldn't really just stand there obtrusively and wait.

So she went back to her own office and rang Max as she had promised she would. Sebastian could come and tell her, she decided. He knew where her office was.

Max answered the phone on the first ring. He was home, but not in a walking cast, and not especially good with his crutches. He was going crazy, he told her. But not entirely because he couldn't get out. Mostly because of who was in his house with him.

"Your mother is driving me nuts," he complained now.

"Is she." Neely didn't make a question. She was staying out of the Max and Lara drama. She'd been doubtful when Lara had insisted on picking Max up at the hospital and taking him home. But no one else had volunteered.

So Lara stepped in. Or rather, showed up.

What happened after that wasn't precisely clear. She may have told Max a few of the home truths she'd threatened to tell him if she could ever get him tied down. He wasn't precisely tied down, but he was on crutches and that seemed to suffice.

Whatever had happened after that, they were still speaking—or yelling—and that was fine with Neely. She had problems enough of her own. The biggest one never came to say he was going out with his father at all. But when she drifted past his office at a little after five, it was to find the door shut and the lights off.

"He already left," Gladys told her.

"Did he say where he was going?"

The older woman shook her head. "He was total Iceman." She cocked her head. "I really thought he was getting over that."

"Not…entirely," Neely said. Under some circumstances she suspected he could be very much The Iceman still.

But he'd made the effort. He'd contacted his father. They were meeting for a drink. She smiled and crossed her fingers. Please God, let it be all right.

She went straight home, wanting to be there when he arrived. Lara called and invited her to come have a meal with her and Max.

"You can referee," her mother said.

"Thank you, no." Neely was adamant about that. She stripped off her work clothes and pulled out a pair of jeans. "I have other things to do."

"I thought you wanted your father and me to get together."

"I never said that!" Next thing you knew she'd be being

blamed for everything in the world. "I simply said I was coming to work out here so I could meet him. I never said you had to take up with him again."

"I wouldn't call what we're doing 'taking up with,'" Lara said tartly.

"What would you call it?"

"Discussing."

"Arguing," she heard Max correct loudly in the background.

"Going over past history," Lara went on as if he hadn't spoken.

"Throwing plates," Max's voice echoed through the phone. He didn't sound too upset, almost…amused.

"You didn't!" Neely said, aghast.

"Only one," Lara said guilelessly. "And not at him. Sure you won't come for a meal?"

"Quite sure, thanks."

Though it might have been entertaining to watch her parents coming to terms with each other—or not—after all these years, Neely wasn't leaving. She even resisted taking Harm for his usual nightly run, instead sticking close to home, where she could see Sebastian's car the minute he pulled in.

But he didn't come.

And didn't come.

Six-thirty turned into seven and seven into eight, and still he didn't appear. At first she worried, but then she told herself not to be silly. Sebastian's not appearing immediately was actually a good thing.

Certainly one drink together would have been enough for him and his father to have discussed Philip's appearance at Vangie's wedding if things were tense. But if they weren't—if father and son had actually hit it off—then one drink could have led to more than one. It could have led to dinner.

Which was probably exactly what it had done, Neely realized when it turned nine and still Sebastian hadn't appeared.

They'd probably decided to have dinner together catching

up, and right this very minute they could be chatting over cups of coffee doing some long-delayed father-son bonding.

Maybe Sebastian had even taken his father over to his penthouse so Philip could spend the evening with the entire family.

All of his brothers and sisters had arrived in Seattle for the wedding. The last of the brothers, a university student called Milos, had come in yesterday afternoon. They'd all been eager to spend time with him. She smiled, thinking how wonderful it would be if his father got to be there with all of them, too.

She wished she could be there to witness it. Unlike her own parents' reunion, she doubted anyone at Sebastian's place would be throwing plates. They were all on their best behavior for the wedding, and judging from what she'd seen of Vangie this afternoon, Sebastian's sister simply wouldn't allow it.

She took a shower a little past ten and came back downstairs eagerly, hoping that he would be home. But only the kittens and Harm were there to greet her. She paced. She prowled. And finally, in desperation, she got down the violin and began to play. And the music, as it always did, settled her, calmed her, reinforced her belief that all would be well.

And when the door finally opened at very nearly midnight, she set it down abruptly and spun around to smile at him when he came in.

He looked like hell.

Actually she didn't suppose he looked a lot different than he looked to most people most days. Stony, silent, serious, supremely self-contained—that was Sebastian ordinarily. That was Sebastian now.

But lately, as Gladys had noticed, the ordinary Iceman Sebastian had thawed a bit. Not just at home, but at work, he'd smiled more. He'd relaxed. He'd been more talkative. He'd even laughed.

Not tonight.

"What happened?"

He stared at her blankly. "Nothing." His voice was toneless.

He shut the door, came into the living room, shrugged off his jacket and sat down. He didn't look her way. One of the kittens started playing with his shoelace. He looked down at it, expression remote. Almost on auto-pilot he reached down and plucked it off, setting it on the back of the sofa.

No chiding it. No smiling. Nothing.

"Seb," she said urgently. "What happened? You saw your father…" she ventured.

There was the faintest stiffening in his demeanor. "Did I?" he said. His tone was conversational, light. But in it she heard the opposite.

"You didn't?"

He gave a quick almost imperceptible shake of his head. "No." He got up and went into the kitchen and with quick almost jerky movements, he poured himself a glass of water and drank it.

Neely watched his Adam's apple work as he swallowed. Tried to read his face. There were lines of strain, a little white bracketing his mouth. When he set the glass down, he shut his eyes, flattened his palms against the countertop and bent his head, dragging in a long harsh breath.

"Seb," she began again. "Tell me—"

He opened his eyes. They were dark, unfathomable. "Tell you what? There's nothing to say." Again that light, almost dismissive tone. A tone that said, it doesn't matter, when his entire being screamed the opposite.

What was she going to do? Was she just going to stand there and let him get away with it? Was she going to pretend to believe his words because he expected her to.

"Yes, there is," she said. "There's plenty to say."

And she came around the bar so that there was no longer a barrier between them. She walked straight up to him, and saw him, for once, retreat a step so that his back was against the cabinet.

He put his hands out as if to ward her off, but she kept coming until she was toe-to-toe with him, until her eyes were on a level with his chin and close enough that her lashes could brush against it.

"Neel'." Her name was a warning, a protest. "You don't want—"

"Yes," she said, "I do." And she was conscious even as she said the words that the vow was there within their meaning.

She put her arms around him, wrapping him tight and felt the hard strength of him when his own arms came around her. He buried his face into her hair, drew in a harsh breath and held it even as he held her. She felt a shudder run through him.

She kissed his neck, his jaw, ran her hands up the solid breadth of his back, and pressed herself even closer, needing the connection, knowing that Sebastian needed it, too.

She didn't know how long they stood there just holding each other in silent communion. And then slowly she become aware of another need—his and hers—a need that had been building for as long as they had been aware of each other.

It was a need she'd rejected, a desire she'd denied—because she hadn't dared believe that anything would come of it.

She'd been afraid to risk. But she had challenged Sebastian to risk. She had been adamant in her insistence that it was worth it. And she knew he had taken that risk tonight, whatever the outcome had been.

And she dared to believe he'd done it for her.

It seemed only fair—only right—to take a risk of her own.

Now she lifted her face to press her lips along his jawline, to find his mouth, to taste his lips with hers.

His fingers curled against her waist. "Neel'—" The warning was there again in his tone.

"Shh," she said. "It's all right."

He drew back to look down at her, his eyes alight with yearning and yet in them she saw still a hint of caution. "Is it?" he asked her. His hands spanned her waist, held her so that their bodies barely brushed. His mouth tightened. His face was taut. A muscle ticked in his jaw.

"Yes," she whispered going up on her toes to brush her lips once more against his, touching them with the tip of her tongue. "Yes, it is."

He believed her then. Took her at her word. Trusted that she knew what she was doing.

She did.

It was a risk. Loving was always a risk. Until Sebastian she hadn't dared.

But she couldn't ask him for a risk she wasn't willing to take.

"I love you," she whispered.

He stiffened, looked down into her eyes. "You don't. You can't." His tone wasn't dismissive any longer. It was as intense as hers.

"Too late." Neely smiled and once more pressed her mouth to his.

"Neel'," Seb protested as she once more wrapped her arms around him and kissed him. But his heart wasn't in it.

Whose would be?

What man in possession of all the proper instincts could possibly be noble enough to walk away from such an offer—such a woman.

He'd craved her, it seemed, forever. Even when he'd believed she was Max's lover, he'd wanted her. And since he had discovered she wasn't, the wanting had, if anything, grown stronger. Learning that she was Max's *daughter* might have tempered it a bit, given him a scruple or two that he wouldn't have had otherwise—but even that had not been enough to turn away from her.

He wanted her. Desperately. Intensely. With every fiber of his being. And he'd give her this one last chance to come to her senses, and if she didn't, she was his.

She didn't.

On the contrary, she was practically climbing inside his shirt.

And Seb almost laughed. "Not here," he murmured. "We're going to do this right."

So saying, he reached down and scooped her up into his arms, then carried her straight down the hall and up the stairs.

"Seb!" She flailed in his arms for a moment, but when he hung on doggedly, she stopped and laughed, shaking her head. "You'll have a heart attack carrying me up the stairs."

"I won't," Seb assured her—and proved it by making it to the top without even breathing hard. "Whose room?"

"Yours," she said without hesitation.

He raised a quizzical brow.

"There're photos of Max and my mother on my dresser. This isn't any business of theirs."

There were no photos on Seb's dresser at all. The room was as austere as his life. It made him a little self-conscious, actually, to let her see it.

He'd never had a woman in his bedroom before. Whenever he'd shared physical intimacies with a woman, it had always been elsewhere, always impersonal. Not especially intimate at all.

With Neely everything was personal, everything was intimate. She wasn't like any other woman he'd ever known. She terrified him. She mesmerized him. She drew him into that intimate world as no one and nothing in his life had ever been able to.

He carried her in and laid her gently on the bed, then turned and pushed the door shut so the dog and cats wouldn't be scandalized. Neely gave him a look of complete understanding, then smiled at him and held out her arms to him.

Seb came down into them. Nothing had ever before felt so right in his life.

He was a good lover. Women he'd been to bed with said so. He took his time, he learned what they liked, gauged their responses, gave them what they wanted. He took his pleasure, too. It was enjoyable. It was first intense and then, in the aftermath, relaxing. It was a shared experience of physical release.

With Neely it was something else entirely.

With Neely it wasn't just about getting her naked, it was about learning the texture of her skin. It was about lifting her shirt and stroking his fingers across her abdomen, thinking he'd never felt anything as soft. It was about tugging that shirt over her head and then cupping his hands around her breasts in their lacy bra and molding them, then with his thumbs bringing her nipples to a peak. It was about bending his head and pressing kisses along the edge of her bra, drawing a line there with his tongue, reveling in the sound of the sharp intake of her breath.

He drew her up so he could release the clasp of her bra and then he stripped it off. Holding the silken mounds in his palms, he pressed kisses to the tips, nuzzled them, savoring the taste, the texture, the soft sounds she made in response.

"My turn," she said, and made quick work of the buttons of his dress shirt. She fumbled with the cuff links—"trust you to make it difficult," she muttered—but she got them in the end. Then she dragged his shirt off him and slid her hands up, cool palms against hot flesh, making him shudder.

He reached up and grasped her hands and put them back on his chest. All the while he was kissing her, nibbling her jawline, tasting her ear, then slipping his fingers beneath her waistband, unfastening her jeans, brushing his hand against her, making her tremble.

"Seb!"

"Mmm." He smiled and eased her jeans down, doing his best to maintain his usual careful control, to make her happy, to see to her needs.

But Neely wouldn't just lie back and let him have his way with her. She had his belt undone, his zip down. Then she scrambled around to pry his shoes and socks off.

"What're you—?"

"You can't make love in your shoes and socks!"

"Can't I?" He laughed.

But she shook her head quite seriously. "No. I want all of you."

He thought she meant she wanted to see all of him—and that was fair enough—he didn't mind being naked with her. She had all that wonderful skin to rub against, to feast on, and to press against his.

But it wasn't just his body she wanted naked.

She gave herself to him—opened her body and her arms and her heart and her soul as she drew him down into the most wonderful warmth he'd ever felt—and as she moved beneath him, he lost all control, all ability to hold back, to give and take on his own terms.

He surged into her as she wrapped herself around him, meeting him thrust for thrust, heartbeat for heartbeat, cry for cry.

And when he shattered, as she did, too, he knew that Neely Robson had got more of him than anyone else ever had.

She got everything he had to give.

That, Neely decided, was the difference between sex and love.

The first was only about the body. The last had no limits. It involved the body, of course. But it was far more than simply taking physical pleasure with another person. It was becoming a part of that person—and of letting them become a part of you.

Scary. Risky. Absolutely wonderful.

And as she lay there savoring the weight of the man she loved as he rested on top of her, she felt a pricking of tears for all the people who were afraid to risk—and for those who risked and lost.

She understood a bit better now the edgy exchanges her parents were having. They had risked. They had loved—and lost. And now they were together for the moment—and very likely terrified of it happening again.

Would they risk? She didn't know.

But she knew she was glad she had. Glad she loved Sebastian. Glad she'd dared to say so and to show him.

Now she ran her fingers lightly over his back, traced the ridge of his spine, then curved her hand against the back of his neck and brushed her fingers against his hairline, learning him physically, loving him totally.

He made a soft sound against her ear, shifted slightly. "'M I too heavy?"

"No." She shook her head. "Never."

He turned his head and she could see the curve of his smile in the moonlight that spilled through the window. "I think I am," he said, and effortlessly rolled them over so that now she lay atop him, though still wrapped in his arms.

"Seb?" She lifted her head to look down at him. Their eyes were bare inches apart. "Will you…tell me…what happened?"

His jaw tightened, and she thought that, if he had stayed on top, he would have pulled away and tried to leave her. But now she stayed right where she was. She leaned forward and lay her cheek next to his.

"Vangie said you were going out for a drink with your father," she prompted.

She didn't think he was going to reply. But then, after what seemed like an eternity, Sebastian said, "Was going." He shifted as if he would have shrugged his shoulders. "He never came."

Once again she heard the tone of light indifference, the one he always used when it was safer and smarter not to acknowledge that it mattered, not to admit the pain.

Neely lifted her gaze and met his again. "His loss," she said.

Sebastian snorted.

But Neely wouldn't dismiss it. "He's a fool," she said as she kissed him again, loving him for the man he'd become without a father's love. "He doesn't deserve you."

It was only the truth.

CHAPTER NINE

IT WAS a perfect day for a wedding.

A storybook sort of day, warm but not sweltering, breezy but not gusting. And there wasn't a cloud in the sky, which, for the Pacific Northwest, was nothing short of amazing.

And one look told Neely that Vangie was going to be a beautiful bride. She was a pretty girl to begin with, but today, with her honey colored hair pulled up into a sophisticated knot, her long white dress elegant and simple and her eyes absolutely sparkling, she looked exquisite and every bit the radiantly happy bride she was.

But she wasn't only happy, she was generous and kind.

Neely had been so proud of her this morning while she was getting ready and Sebastian came in. Despite her mother and step-mothers wringing their hands and trying to make her stay right where she was so they could get her train arranged just so, Vangie had dashed across the room to throw her arms around her brother.

"Thank you," she said. "I didn't say it the other day, but I should have. Thank you for trying…for trying to talk to Daddy and—" she stepped back and, still clasping his hands in hers, looked up at him with a tremulous smile "—for everything. You are the best."

He was the best. Neely knew that. And she loved him for the smile he had managed for Vangie.

"Anything I can do for you," he'd said. And Neely knew—they all knew—it was nothing more than the truth. Even though he hadn't been able to produce their father, he'd done everything else.

While he'd obviously been the one his sister had turned to for months, this week it became crystal clear that he was the one the whole family turned to as well.

He was always willing to talk to them and listen to them—whether it was about Vangie's silver and rose mint boxes or which medical schools Milos should apply to. He listened to his stepmother Gina fret about his brother Gabriel's umpteen girl-friends and he spent a morning taking his youngest sister to the office and to a couple of his job sites so she could learn what being an architect entailed.

He managed to defuse half a dozen wedding-related crises as well. He was the one who stepped in and arranged for the limo when the one Garrett had contacted had a conflict. He was the one who saw to it that all his stepmothers had corsages when nobody else had. This morning he was the one who tied all his brothers' ties.

And right after they got out of the car, he'd said to Neely, "Stand still." And he used masking tape to go over her dress and make sure there was no lingering rabbit or kitten or dog hair on Neely's dress.

"A master of details," she'd teased him, grinning.

He'd smiled that crooked half smile of his and said, "Someone's got to do it."

Neely understood now that that someone was always Sebastian.

And now she sat with the wedding guests in rows of white chairs on the lawn overlooking the sound, waiting to watch him do yet another task—this one a task he had every right to—walking his sister down the aisle and giving her to her groom.

She hoped he would smile when he did so. He had the most beautiful smile. She wasn't treated to it often. But he'd smiled at her the night they'd made love. He'd smiled that smile the next morning when he'd awakened with his arms around her.

And she dared to hope that she would see that same amazing smile someday soon at their wedding when he watched her walk down an aisle toward him.

Still, it was too soon to think about that.

The string quintet—one of the few things Sebastian had not had a hand in arranging—began at that moment to play the processional. Neely stood and turned with everyone else to watch as the bridesmaids proceeded in measured steps across the grass to where a handsome nervous Garrett and his grinning best man waited with the minister.

Little Sarah came first, her head high, her eyes straight ahead, her expression solemn, but every now and then Neely saw a flicker of a smile very like Sebastian's on her face. Then came Jenna, her ash-blonde hair a striking contrast to the rest of the girls. The triplets—Ariadne, Alexa and Anastasia—followed. Neely still had no idea which was which, but Sebastian never seemed to have trouble telling them apart.

"Not now I don't," he'd said when she'd marveled at his ability. "But when they were little it was like three little indistinguishable dark-haired devils. Seriously scary."

There was a pause in the music after the last of the triplets had reached the halfway mark of the procession, and then the quintet picked up the volume and plunged into the bridal music once more.

Everyone turned and twisted their heads and craned their necks to get their first glimpse of the bride.

Everyone except Neely. She was twisting her head and craning her neck to catch a first glimpse of Sebastian resplendent in black tie, white shirt and tuxedo jacket.

So she was poleaxed to see an older, craggier tuxedo-clad Savas male walking with Vangie up the path instead!

The bride was absolutely radiant, beaming at everyone, looking from side to side as she walked slowly toward her waiting groom. And the man was smiling happily and looking at her dotingly—as if he had a right to be there.

In one way, she supposed he did. She knew exactly who he was—Phillip Savas, the man who had given her life. He was her father in name. But who had been there for her every single day?

She looked around desperately for Sebastian. *Where was he?*

Not with his sister, that was certain. She had her father to give her away just as she'd wanted.

The way it should be.

Neely could hear the words echoing in her brain. They were the words Vangie had used. And Sebastian had reiterated them even as he'd refused at first to make the effort.

"She wants a normal wedding. A normal family," he'd said. "That's all she's ever wanted."

And this was what she wanted? A father who showed up for a few brief moments and stepped in at the last minute to give her away? As if it were his right when in fact he'd really given her away years ago!

It wasn't his right! Neely was outraged. How dared he? Where had he come from?

And most important of all, *Where was Sebastian?*

She should have been watching the ceremony. But she barely noticed that Philip had handed his daughter off to Garrett and had gone to stand by his string of ex-wives. She was craning her neck trying to find Sebastian.

Ah, there. At the very back she spotted his dark head. He was perfectly composed, though she was sure she wouldn't have been. He stood ramrod straight, looking for all the world like one of the ushers and not the man who had every right to have walked his sister up the aisle.

The wedding was short and sweet—at least Neely supposed it was. She barely noticed. Her mind was consumed with indignation for Sebastian, with annoyance toward his father. No one else seemed to notice.

The Savases looked like a normal family on the eldest daughter's wedding day: mother with a tear-streaked smiling face, father beaming as he bestowed her hand on her groom, the bride joyful, the groom solemn.

And where the eldest brother was no one cared.

Except her.

Neely cared. And she barely waited until after the ceremony to slip away and go to him. But when she looked around, he wasn't there. Vangie and Garrett, his parents and hers were in a reception line and everyone was lined up to go past and congratulate them.

Sebastian should have been there, too. If anyone deserved congratulations for getting Vangie married it was him. But she didn't see him anywhere. She could have waited in the reception line and asked Vangie, but judging from the happily dazed expression on Vangie's face, she wouldn't have known.

She did ask Gabriel, "Where's your brother?"

But Gabriel just shrugged and looked blank. So did Milos and the triplets. "He's around somewhere," Jenna said, waving her hand toward the hundreds of people milling about on the lawn.

It was Sarah who pointed. "He's over there."

Following her pointing finger, Neely spied Sebastian on the far side of the gathering. He was standing with a couple she'd never seen before. They were talking and he was listening. He had his hands tucked into the pockets of his black trousers. His dark head was bent.

He didn't look shattered. He looked perfectly fine. But Neely couldn't help cutting through the crowds of people to get to him.

"Ah, there you are!" She smiled brilliantly as she came up to him, and he lifted his gaze and smiled. It wasn't the best Sebastian Savas smile, the one that could curl her toes. But it was warm and welcoming and he reached out a hand and drew her to him, looping an arm over her shoulders.

"This is Neely Robson," he told the other couple, and to Neely he said, "My cousin Theo and his wife, Martha."

He introduced her to more cousins and aunts and uncles, and was completely affable and pleasant. He never once mentioned

his father, never said a word about the switch. Of course she knew
Sebastian well enough that she didn't expect him to make a fuss
about it, but she thought he might say something to her in the
few moments they were alone.

But when they were alone he stole a kiss, and while it was a
perfectly discreet kiss in public, it meant she didn't get to find
out what happened.

"Are you all right?" she asked him briefly.

He blinked, surprised. "I'm fine."

"Your father—"

But Sebastian simply turned away. "Let's get something to eat."

They got something to eat. They talked to a myriad Savas aunts,
uncles, cousins and friends. Sebastian was perfectly polite, completely composed. He didn't seem like an Iceman on the surface—
not the way he used to appear at work sometimes—but beneath
the surface charm, Neely began to suspect that the ice was there.

She caught a sense of it in his tone of voice. It was that easy,
polite and on-the-surface-pleasant tone, yet there was in it, too,
a distance, a determined emotional detachment.

Yes, Sebastian agreed with everyone who said so, Vangie was
a beautiful bride and Garrett was a lucky man. He allowed that
it was terrific that their whole family could be here. And he even
nodded and said, yes, wasn't it nice that they all—even the ex-
wives—got on so well.

"Philip always did know how to pick 'em," his father's older
brother, Socrates, said cheerfully. Socrates's son, Theo, winced
at the comment, but Sebastian didn't bat an eye.

But he wasn't, Neely started to understand as time went on,
quite as sanguine as he seemed. It was unobtrusive but apparent,
to her at least—though she was sure she was the only one who
noticed—that he was careful to keep a couple hundred people
between himself and his father at all times.

Not that it was difficult. Philip Savas was clearly a charming,
gregarious man. He was every bit as handsome as his son with

a more affable outgoing manner. In situations like this Sebastian was pleasant but quiet. He didn't have the innate ease his father did with social settings. Wherever Philip went, people were smiling and laughing, beaming at him, shaking his hand, clapping him on the back.

His children—except for Sebastian—flocked around him, eager for fatherly attention. Even his ex-wives seemed to preen under his benevolent eye.

Philip was in his element. He paid attention to them all, charmed them all—his oft-neglected family, the multitude of wedding guests and, of course, Garrett's family as well. Her father's presence and his behavior was everything Vangie had wanted.

Neely found it interesting, though, that even as he conversed with all of them, his gaze kept shifting toward Sebastian. At first she thought she might have imagined it. But the more she watched, the more often she saw Philip's glance move their way. As he chatted his way from group to group, he seemed to be edging closer and closer to his eldest son.

Sebastian never looked his way. He kept a possessive hand on Neely's arm or looped his over her shoulders, but his focus was on whichever friend, relative or guest was talking with him.

And yet, somehow, without Neely quite realizing how, Sebastian managed to move them further away. It was a dance of pursuit and avoidance. Never directly acknowledged by father or son.

Once Philip caught her eye and smiled at her. She supposed it was even a genuine smile, but it couldn't hold a candle to his son's. She didn't smile back, but she did say to Sebastian, "I think your father wants to talk to you."

But Sebastian acted like he didn't hear, instead spinning her onto the small dance floor and taking her in his arms. "Let's dance."

Oh, yes. It was a slow dance, one that allowed Neely to loop her arms around his neck while his held her close to his chest. They moved together, swayed, shifted, shuffled.

Neely closed her eyes and rested her head on his shoulder, breathing in the scent of him—the piney aftershave, the starch of his shirt, a hint of the sea, something uniquely Sebastian. She felt the touch of his lips to her hair, felt his arms tighten around her. And she savored it, stored away the moment and knew she would always remember this.

"May I cut in?"

Neely's head jerked up as Sebastian's arms went stiff around her. They both looked around to see Philip just behind Sebastian, his hand raised from apparently having tapped his son's shoulder, a hopeful smile on his handsome face.

Sebastian seemed to turn to stone. He had certainly stopped breathing. Neely breathed, but what she was breathing was righteous anger at the same time she realized that there was no way she could make a scene in the middle of Vangie's wedding.

Everything had been picture perfect so far. She couldn't ruin it by telling Sebastian's father exactly what she thought of him. And even more clearly she couldn't allow Sebastian to do what she suspected he itched to do. Not that she blamed him.

But punching out his father's lights in the middle of his sister's wedding was not the "normal" family behavior that would endear him to Vangie—or anyone else.

She unclasped her fingers and stroked the back of his neck. He didn't speak, didn't even move—except for the tick of a muscle in his jaw and a sort of vibrato tremor that ran through his limbs.

Neely ran her hand down his arm and smiled her best well-brought-up smile. "How do you do?" she said. "I'm Neely Robson. And you must be Mr. Savas." She did not say, *You must be Sebastian's father.*

"Call me Philip," the older man said. He glanced at Sebastian. "I'm sure you don't mind if I make the acquaintance of your lovely friend."

"Sebastian and I are living together," Neely said firmly. So maybe not in the traditional sense, but she wanted it clear they were not merely friends. As if anyone could think so given the way they'd been dancing.

"Of course," Philip said genially. "My son doesn't believe in marriage."

"I wonder why," Sebastian said through his teeth. They were the first words he'd spoken since Philip had cut in.

Philip only laughed. "Well, I promise not to propose to Miss Robson. How about that?" His tone was light and jokey but what was going on between them was no laughing matter.

"Don't worry. I'd say no," Neely said in an equally light tone. But just as she did so, the music ended, and she breathed a sigh of relief, thinking the whole problem might have been avoided.

But the quintet immediately went into the next number and Philip held out a hand to her. "This one will be mine, then, I think."

Sebastian didn't move. His fingers curled into a fist. Neely pressed her hand down on his arm. "One dance, Mr. Savas," she said evenly. And she gave Sebastian's forearm a squeeze.

He looked at her hand on his arm, then he raised his gaze to hers, his eyes as hard as green granite, his mouth flat and uncompromising.

Neely pressed her own lips together and raised her eyebrows, then suggested gently. "Why don't you dance with Vangie? I'll bet she'd like that."

Sebastian's jaw seemed locked. Only his eyes moved—from her to his father, then back again.

But finally he gave a curt nod and released her. "Enjoy yourself."

He should have known.

It was just like Philip to breeze in at the last minute and act like he'd meant to be there all along.

"Got delayed in Japan," was all he'd said.

"For *four* days?" Sebastian couldn't mask his disbelief.

But of course it didn't matter. Daddy was here now, and that was what mattered to Vangie. To his brothers and sisters. To all the stupid stepmothers. To everyone.

Except him.

And he frankly didn't give a damn.

Now he stalked across the dance floor to the table where his sister sat with Garrett. "Dance with me."

She had danced with her husband, her father (of course) and Garrett's father. But then she had sat down, preferring to simply watch and share the day with her husband. But now she looked up, startled, then smiled up at Seb, delighted. "Of course. We didn't get to before, did we?"

Before—when they'd been supposed to follow Vangie and Garret's bridal waltz, Philip had danced with her instead.

"No," Seb said shortly and held out a hand to her. Beaming, she took the floor with him.

Over her head he could see his father smiling and talking to Neely. He was going all out to charm her. Sebastian recognized all the moves, the flatteringly intent expression, the easy flirtatiousness.

Neely's back was to him, so Seb wasn't able to gauge her reaction. But his father had never failed to win a woman over yet.

He hadn't expected Philip to cut in on them. He should have, he supposed. It was the sort of blatant, flagrant attention-seeking thing his father would do. Seb knew he should have seen it coming when Philip kept trying to catch his eye, as if they had something to say to each other.

He'd ignored it because he had nothing to say to Philip. And whatever his father might have to say, Sebastian had no desire to listen.

Now he didn't have to talk to Sebastian. He had a more malleable captive audience. And clearly he was making the most of it. He was a better dancer than his son and he twirled Neely in his arms and spun her around and she laughed.

Sebastian stepped on Vangie's foot. "Sorry."

"It's all right." Vangie was in a mood to be pleased by everything. "It's been a gorgeous wonderful day, hasn't it?"

"Mm." He could see Neely talking now. Philip's brows lifted, he opened his mouth, then shut it again. Neely kept talking.

"I couldn't believe it when Daddy showed up. Thank you for that."

"Me? I didn't do it." God forbid.

"You tried," Vangie said. "He told me he got your message. Told me you said he should be here."

"He never responded."

"Yes, he did," Vangie said happily. "He came."

And as always, just like bloody Caesar, Philip saw and then he conquered.

Seb's jaw grew tight. He tensed as he watched Philip spin Neely round again, then start talking while Neely cocked her head and listened.

Was this song never going to end?

Then he heard Neely's laughter. He turned his head to see her smiling up into his father's eyes. He stopped dead.

Vangie tripped over his feet. "Sorry," she said. "My fault."

"No." But he couldn't do this anymore. "Let me take you back so you can sit down before I walk all over you."

He took her arm and steered her back to Garrett before the music even ended. She sat down and looked up at him to smile again. "Thanks, Seb. For everything."

"For stepping on your feet." He smiled wryly as the music finally came to an end and Neely still stood with his father on the far side of the dance floor deep in conversation. Then she smiled, nodded and Philip leaned in and kissed her on the cheek.

Vangie squeezed his hands, drawing his attention back to her. "No. Thanks for making my dreams come true."

"You're welcome," he said because it was the right thing to do.

Some people's dreams did come true, he supposed as he walked away.

Frankly Seb found it hard to imagine.

"It was the most beautiful wedding I've ever been to," Neely said on their way home.

"Uh-huh."

She slanted him a glance. His gaze was, of course, on the road. It was late—past eleven—and they were exhausted, but fortunately they were nearly home. She'd been carrying the conversation all the way. Sebastian's contributions had, like the last one, been delivered in single syllables and a monotone.

Of course he'd done so much to make it a great day for his sister that she didn't expect him to talk a lot. But he'd been increasingly quiet, not just since they'd left the reception but since the dance his father had cut in on.

Now, as he turned down the hill to the parking area by the dock, she said quietly, "It's actually hard to hate him."

She didn't say whom. She knew she didn't have to.

Sebastian's fingers tightened on the steering wheel. "I wouldn't know." His tone was cold.

At least, Neely thought, it wasn't that light dismissive tone that made her crazy.

"You don't hate him," she said with more confidence than she felt.

"I don't give a damn about him," Sebastian said roughly. He turned into a parking space and cut the engine.

"Not true."

His jaw worked. In the streetlight she could see his knuckles whiten as his fingers clenched.

"He wanted to talk to you, not me," Neely said quietly.

He didn't look at her, just stared straight ahead. "He could have talked to me four days ago."

"He really did get delayed in Japan."

Sebastian slapped his hands on the steering wheel. "Don't make excuses for him!"

"I'm *not* making excuses!"

"No?" He turned to glare at her. "What do you call it?"

"Sanity?" she suggested. "Common sense?"

"To believe everything he tells you? To let yourself be conned?"

"I'm *not* letting myself be conned! He said he wanted to apologize. You wouldn't let him get close." That was more or less what he had said. Plus he'd said he wanted to get to know the woman who seemed to have captured his oldest son's heart.

Of course she didn't say that now.

Sebastian was already snorting his disbelief at what she did say. He jerked open the car door and came around to open hers, but Neely got out by herself and stalked down the dock toward the houseboat.

Sebastian caught up with her. "I don't want him close," he said flatly.

"I think you made that perfectly clear. Look," she said, rounding on him by their front door, "I'm not condoning your father's behavior. I think it stinks, but—"

"Did you tell him that? You didn't, did you?" he demanded furiously. "Of course you didn't! You're just like all the rest!"

He stuck his key in the lock and shoved the door open. Harm bounded up to meet them. Kittens tumbled sleepily down the stairs. Sebastian ignored them all, just held the door and simultaneously glowered accusingly at her.

Disregarding her dress and everything but the pain in her heart and the tears that stung her eyes, Neely marched past him and knelt to wrap her arms around the dog. She hugged him hard, pressed her face into his short soft fur. Drew a breath. Drew strength.

Then she stood again and turned to face Sebastian. "I did, you know,"

He stared. "Did what?"

"Told him it stunk, what he'd done. Told him he hurt you. Told him what a jerk he was." She glared at him defiantly.

Sebastian looked stunned. And then he shook his head in disbelief. "Sure you did. That's why he was laughing. Why you were! Why he danced you around and kissed your cheek!"

There was a short silence and then she said, "You don't believe me."

He hunched his shoulder. "I saw what I saw."

She slowly shook her head. "No, you saw what you wanted to see."

He didn't say anything, just stared stonily at her.

"You don't believe me. You don't trust me." Neely felt cold. She felt gutted. She felt as if her determined and furious attack on Sebastian's father, which he had certainly not been expecting when he'd asked for a dance, had all been for naught.

She'd had to give Philip credit. He'd first looked as stunned as Sebastian when she'd told him what she thought of him. But he'd listened. He'd shut his mouth and heard her out. And then he'd talked.

Of course she hadn't believed every word he said. Of course she knew a sound byte when she heard one. But she also heard some truth in the desperation Philip Savas had expressed. She'd heard a man who had made a mess of most of the relationships in his life, a man who'd lost the respect of his eldest son and knew it. She heard a man who could be both self-aware and self-deprecating, a man who understood his own weaknesses but who hadn't yet figured out how to compensate for them.

By the end of the dance yes, they'd laughed. But it had been equally tempting to cry—for him and for his son.

"Don't tell me my father didn't try to bring you around to his way of thinking," Sebastian said grimly.

"Of course he did. In his ham-handed way, he wants you in his life. He wants us to design a hotel for him."

"Oh, for God's sake! As if I would ever—"

"You could," Neely said stubbornly. "We could."

Sebastian shook his head. "I'll never! And you won't either if you want whatever we've got between us to work."

"What do we have between us, Seb?" she asked. She was almost afraid to, not really wanting to face the answer. "Do we have love? Commitment? Forever?"

His jaw tightened. "We have a good thing. You know that."

"I thought so," Neely agreed slowly. "Now I'm not so sure."

He raked a hand through his hair. "Why not? Because I won't knuckle under to my perennially absent father's demand?"

Neely shook her head. "This isn't about your father."

"No? Then what is it about?"

"It's about whether you're ever going to trust me to be on your side. Even when I challenge you, I'm still on your side. But you didn't believe I'd be there for you with Carmody, either."

"This isn't about Carmody!"

"No, it isn't. It's about trust, Sebastian."

He shook his head. "If that's the way you feel, we don't have anything else to say. I'm giving you everything I've got," he said flatly. "I can't give you any more."

"Can't?" Neely said quietly, looking at him and feeling her heart breaking. "Or won't?"

CHAPTER TEN

HE LEFT.

Neely heard him go.

She had run up to her bedroom and shut the door and prayed that he would come after her. But there were no footsteps on the stairs. There was no light knock on her door. There was no sound of her name.

There was only silence—and then the front door opening and closing.

She ran to the window and looked out to see him walking up the dock. He looked weary and exhausted and alone, and she wanted nothing so much as to call to him, to tell him to come back and to wrap her arms around him and tell him she loved him.

But if she did, he wouldn't believe her. He didn't trust her, didn't trust her word.

So he couldn't—or wouldn't—believe she loved him.

He kept walking until he disappeared into the darkness. Moments later an engine started, headlights came on. A car backed out and turned to go up the hill.

He drove away.

She was mad. She'd get over it.

Neely wasn't silly. She had to see that they were good together. And she had to know it wasn't worth throwing away over nothing.

He gave her the weekend to come to her senses. In the meantime, he made his sisters double up, his brothers take the sofas, and he moved back into his penthouse. It was a madhouse. Noise, clutter, commotion. It should have taken his mind off her.

It might have if they hadn't all asked, "Where's Neely?" and "What are you doing here?"

"I live here," he said shortly.

But as he took them one by one to the airport over the next day and a half and got his penthouse back, he didn't feel as if he lived there anymore. The penthouse didn't feel like home at all.

Home was where Neely was.

Tuesday evening he spent the day listening to Roger Carmody sing Neely's praises once again—"Makes complete sense, that girl. Got a feel for what makes people tick. Made sense of all that soaring space you like so much. Good thing you sent her to talk to me."

"She's very astute," Seb said in his best politic manner.

Now he hoped she was astute enough to have come to her senses. He'd missed her. He was ready to let bygones be bygones. So he went home.

And when he parked his car and went down the steps to the dock, despite his earlier anger, he felt that increasingly familiar sense of anticipation, of the eagerness he always felt when he was coming home to the houseboat.

To Neely.

Of course she wouldn't be home yet. He'd left Carmody early and she'd still be at work. But that would give him a chance to be there first, to surprise her.

He opened the door, prepared now for Harm's immediate dash and skid around the corner from the living room. He was already grinning in anticipation.

But the entry was silent and empty.

"Harm! Hey, buddy! Where are you?"

Seb supposed the dog could be out on the deck. It was a sunny day. He liked to lie in the sun's warmth. Or maybe Cody had come to take him running if Neely knew she was going to be late. A glance toward the hook told him that Harm's leash was gone.

But so was his food dish. And his water bowl.

Seb's stomach did a slow awful somersault and ended feeling as if it had lodged in his throat.

"Harm?" He called the dog's name louder now, an edge to his voice. A new unwelcome feeling settled in his chest.

Apprehension? Worry? Panic?

No, he thought. *No!*

But all the same, he strode quickly down the hall into the living area. The sofa was there, and the armchair, the lamps, the desk with his computer, the bookshelves.

But only half the books were there. His half.

The rocker Max had made Neely was gone. So was the afghan he knew her mother had knitted her.

And the coffee table that had been in front of the sofa—the one with the drawers for architectural drawings, the one that Neely had talked Max out of, her pride and joy, the one she wouldn't let him set his boxes on when he'd first moved in—that was gone, too.

Max could have taken it back, Seb told himself. Neely had said she was "trying it out" to see if it was the one she wanted or if she wanted Max to make her something else.

"Anything I want, he said," she'd told Seb. "But that's silly. He knows very well I want this one."

And Seb knew it hadn't gone back to Max.

It had simply gone.

Like Harm. And the kittens. And—he looked around desperately, hardly able to breathe—the rabbits and the guinea pig.

Gone. All gone. With Neely.

"The Iceman is back."

Seb heard Gladys mutter the words under her breath to Danny when Seb snapped at one of her questions. He stiffened, but ignored it, just as he had ignored every curious look and leading question the past five days.

It wasn't any of their business. He worked with them. He didn't owe them explanations.

If they wanted explanations, damn it, they could ask Neely.

But Neely wasn't here.

"She's out of town. She's taken on another project," Max had reported when Seb had rang him, demanding to know where the hell she was.

"And she took all her books and her furniture?" Seb said before he could stop himself.

"Did she?" Max said. "Mmm. Interesting."

That wasn't the term Seb would have used.

He had given up being gutted about personal relationships gone awry about the time his father had split with his third wife.

It didn't do to get close. It didn't do to try to make something more out of what was clearly going to be no more than a brief encounter.

Oh, sure, his new stepmothers might have promised "forever" but it hadn't taken Seb long to learn that it never lasted. They grew weary of Philip's absences, his distractions, his inability to get involved. And they left.

They took their children with them and made new lives for themselves. But they never took Sebastian because Sebastian wasn't theirs.

He only belonged to Philip—and Philip didn't care.

No one cared.

Three stark words that cut to the core of his soul.

For years Seb hadn't let it matter. Though at times the knowledge pressed against the inside of his head, making it throb, had clogged his throat, making it ache, he'd ignored it, put it aside, soldiered on.

He'd been wounded by his father's neglect, but he'd survived because he'd refused to care enough—to love enough—to let it hurt.

But all the resolve in the world was no proof against this pain. This emptiness.

This was different. This wasn't his childhood. This wasn't his past. He was an adult. He was over all that. This was now.

This was Neely. And there was no way to fight against her leaving him. No way to turn his back, to say it didn't matter.

Because it did.

Because, God help him, he was in love with her.

Fiercely Seb shook his head. Fought it off, lied to himself, told himself he didn't love her. Couldn't. Wouldn't.

"Can't, Seb?" she'd said coolly. "Or won't?"

He hated the challenge that echoed in his mind. He fought it off. Denied it.

He *wouldn't* love her. Or if he already did, damn it, he'd stop.

It would be all right. He would get by. There was nothing wrong with being an iceman. It was a hell of a lot safer. Saner. Less painful.

He'd cope.

He threw himself into his work. He spent hours overseeing every single detail of the Blake-Carmody project. If Neely wasn't going to be there to do her part, so be it. He'd do it himself.

He wondered what other project could possibly be more important, that Max would have sent her off now, but he didn't ask.

He didn't want to know. Max worked from home and Seb worked in the office and in the field. When he had questions on Blake-Carmody, he asked Danny or Frank or he got Gladys to call her.

"Don't you have her number?" Gladys asked.

"I don't have time. Just get the answers and put it in a memo," Seb said.

He didn't want to talk to her. It still hurt too much.

He left the houseboat and moved back to his penthouse. It was what he'd intended all along, wasn't it? The houseboat had been a stopgap, just until the wedding was over. Now he had his place back—all to himself.

The pizza boxes were gone. So were the panty hose. The bathroom countertops had been swept clean of nail polish, hair spray bottles, foundation, powder, lipstick and mascara.

He didn't step on plastic soda bottles or tortilla chips. He didn't see any remnants of his sisters' occupation after his cleaner blitzed her way through the place. And if there was a lingering odor of overly cloying cologne in the rooms, he could leave the windows open and it would vanish within days.

Everything went back to being exactly the way he'd left it.

Only he had changed.

Now he stood in his spare austere living room with its view across the skyline to the sound and didn't relish the view anymore. Or not as much as he had in the past.

It seemed too remote. Too far above things. Too impersonal.

It made him long for the little houseboat on the water. It made him want a kitten leaping out at his shoelaces when he walked into the kitchen. It made him want a dog smiling a doggy smile and thumping its tail when he walked in the door. He wouldn't even mind if it shed on his navy suit coat.

He had no one to talk to. No one to share a meal with.

He had no one at all.

Jenna was the first of his sisters to call him.

"How are you?" she asked, which surprised him. Usually she only called when she wanted something and it was the first thing she said. But while he waited, the expected request never came.

"I had such a good time with you," she said. "It was fun being a family, being together. I thought I might come back," she said. "To go to the university. If that's okay with you?"

"If you want," Seb said, wondering where this had come from and waited again for the request for money or advice. But Jenna only said, "Can you have cats in the dorms, I wonder."

"I doubt it," Seb said. "Who cares? You don't have a cat."

"I do. Her name is Chloe. Neely gave her to me."

Seb felt as if he'd been punched in the gut. "*Neely* gave you a cat?"

One of *their* kittens?

"Mmm-hmm." Jenna sounded thrilled. "She said she needed to find homes for them. They were getting big enough. We all have them."

"*What?*"

"She gave us each one."

So, the triplets and Sarah each had one of Neely's cats?

"And Marisa took the guinea pig," Jenna told him gaily. That was Sarah's mother.

"Yeah?" Seb wondered who got the rabbits. And Harm. He didn't ask.

"She said she wanted us to have a part of her," Jenna reported.

But she hadn't wanted him to have a part of her.

Or did she think he wouldn't want one?

The next day he bought a fish. Neely had once said she had started with a fish. They'd been sitting on the deck one evening and she'd told him about her first pet.

"I had a fish because fish are portable. Easier to take when we moved. And they don't run away back to where they've been. They're there for you."

Like Neely had been.

He knew that now. There was no way to deny it. And as time passed he didn't want to. He fed his fish and cared for his fish.

But frankly he thought the fish looked lonely. So two days later he bought another fish.

Maybe they'd have little fish. Or one would eat the other.

He wondered which.

Would Neely know?

"It's nearly midnight!" Max, hair ruffled and wearing what looked like hastily pulled-on shorts over his cast, leaned on his crutches and scowled furiously at Seb when he opened the door. "You might work at all hours, but some of us like a little time off now and then."

"I'm taking time off," Seb said gruffly, brushing past Max heading straight into the living room without waiting for an invitation. "But first I need to know where Neely is."

He turned and waited while Max crutched his way into the living room, sputtering and looking indignant. "What do you care where she is?"

"I need to talk to her. And don't ask me about what. That's between your daughter and me!"

Max's brows shot up, but he didn't answer at once, just looked Seb over sceptically.

Seb waited. He'd wait till kingdom come if necessary.

"She's with your old man," Max told him.

It was a blow. Seb felt his teeth come together, but he forced himself to simply nod. "Her choice," he said evenly.

Max's brows lifted. "One you didn't agree with."

"No." No use arguing that. "I didn't." He took a breath. "I've changed my mind."

Now Max's eyes really did go wide. But before he could reply, a husky female voice spoke up. "About time."

Seb looked up to see Neely's mother standing on the landing clad in what had to be Max's bathrobe and little else. Obviously there was more going on here than simple nursing care.

"Give him the address, Max," she said. "He looks ghastly."

"Maybe she won't want to see him," Max said.

"Up to her. At least he's going after her," Neely's mother said pointedly. "Which is more than you ever did."

Max grimaced and rubbed a hand against the back of his neck. "Well, you know how it is. Some of us take longer to wise up." He copied an address down and handed it to Seb. "Good luck."

"You'll need it," Lara added.

Seb had no doubt about that.

* * *

The cabin was in the middle of nowhere. Admittedly it was the most beautiful bit of nowhere that Neely had ever been in—a balm to the most troubled soul—and good thing because she needed all the balm she could get.

She stopped now to stare out the window at the expanse of Lake Chelan through the trees. She drew on the view for inspiration as she tried to bring the outside in—to capture the grandeur that Sebastian did so well in his soaring spaces and expanses of glass, while at the same time trying to create the sense of safe harbor, of peaceful retreat that her own heart sought.

Finding the balance between the two was the hardest work she'd ever done. Particularly because half the time she wasn't even sure she should be here.

Neely knew perfectly well that Philip had only asked her because he really wanted his son to do it. He'd been perfectly polite and welcoming when she'd shown up instead.

He'd been a little wary of course. "Does Sebastian know you're here?" he'd asked her the afternoon she'd come to discuss the idea.

Neely had had to admit he didn't. "We didn't exactly see eye to eye on things."

Philip wasn't clueless. "He doesn't want anything to do with me."

Neely rather thought that Sebastian felt Philip had never wanted anything to do with him. But she only said that she had discussed it with Max, and if Philip was interested in having her work on a design, she would be happy to do it.

She'd brought him a portfolio of her other work, and he'd been impressed enough to agree. Over the past two and a half weeks, she had worked with him almost every day, exploring the site, listening to his ideas, creating sketches and working out plans.

It was intense and creative and energizing—exactly the sort of time that would have gone a long way toward healing the rift between Philip and his son—if his son had deigned to come.

She hadn't seen Seb or heard from him since he'd stalked out of the houseboat the night of Vangie's wedding.

She'd waited. And waited. Had wanted to talk, to discuss, to explain. But when he hadn't come back she realized he didn't intend to.

No doubt he'd simply moved back to the penthouse and taken up his old life right where he'd left off. Without her.

Still, when she'd packed up her furniture, her books and her animals, Neely had dared to hope he would come after her.

She knew she loved him.

And despite his resistence, despite his reluctance to trust, she believed, deep down, that he loved her.

She stared at the boat cruising up the lake and wondered if Philip would be here soon. He came most afternoons and they reworked the sketches she came up with the day before. He was easy to talk to, warm and engaging, yet always edgy and on the move. There wasn't the peace in him that she saw in his son.

Peace? In Sebastian?

Maybe not always. But she dared to believe that he'd found a little with her.

Would that peace have been enough? Certainly she could have stayed—could have simply shared his bed and his house-boat and taken what he thought he could give.

And they would have had great sex and also a certain degree of contentment.

But it wasn't enough. Just as her mother had never been able to accept the little Max had been willing to give years ago, Neely knew she wanted more than great sex, a bit of peace and con-tentment with Sebastian.

She wanted everything. She wanted the love and connection that her parents finally seemed to be finding with each other now. Max and Lara together at last. Who'd have thought it?

It just proved, Neely supposed, that it was never too late.

But she couldn't imagine waiting another twenty-seven years

or so for Seb. After three weeks and not a word, not a sign—nothing at all—she didn't expect there was any point.

She reached her toe out and nudged her sleeping dog. "You're here for me, aren't you?"

Harm opened one eye and closed it again. So much for that.

She forced her attention back to the sketch she was working on. It was for the lobby area of what would be a fifteen-room inn. "Small and intimate, yes," Philip had said, "but with light and space. Bring the outside in."

He sounded just like his son.

Neely chewed on her pencil and tried to think how to convey exactly that when Harm jumped up and went barking to the door.

"It's just Philip," she said. "Don't fuss."

Usually Harm didn't. But he was barking his head off today. "Stop it, you stupid dog!" Neely got up and jerked open the door. "See! It's just—"

Sebastian.

She stared. Not Philip at all. His son. Lean and dark and as serious looking as ever Neely had seen him. Every bit as gorgeous, too, in a pair of faded blue jeans and a long-sleeved grey shirt.

The Iceman? Or not?

Harm flung himself onto Sebastian who scratched his ears and rubbed his fur and grinned broadly at him, making Neely want to fling herself at him as well.

She didn't because she didn't know why he was there.

For all she knew Max had sent him up here on some wild-goose chase. That would be just like Max—he was turning into an unrelenting romantic.

"Harm, get down!" she said, trying to tug the dog back.

But Sebastian just said, "It's all right. I've missed him." And then his grin faded and their eyes met and Neely thought she might drown in the depths of them before he said, "I've missed you."

There was a ragged edge to his voice she hadn't heard before.

This wasn't The Iceman, then. She wet her lips. Her fingers gripped the handle of the door.

"Can I come in?"

She nodded and stepped back, waiting until he came in, and she shut the door to ask, "Is something wrong? Are Max and Lara—?"

"They're fine. Together, apparently." He sounded a little dazed at that.

"Yes," Neely said. "They might make it this time. They have a ways to go, though."

"But they're taking a chance."

She nodded again. He was so close. She could see the pulse beat in his throat and wanted to reach out a finger and touch it. She could see whiskers on his jaw and wanted to rub her cheek against them, feeling them rough one way and smooth the other. She wanted—

"Will you take a chance on me?"

Sometimes in the forest all sound stopped. The birds hushed. The wind dropped. Nothing sounded. No one moved. It was like that now.

"Your father—"

"This is not about my father," Seb said firmly just as she had said it to him. But as he spoke there was a ghost of a smile on his lips. "But if you must know, he says you have to make up your own mind."

"He—" Neely stared. "You talked to him?"

Sebastian shrugged. "How do you think I found you?"

Abruptly Neely sat down. Her mind spun. He had come after her? He had talked to his father?

"He says you do wonderful warm and cozy," Sebastian told her, "but that you're struggling a bit with the light and space."

"He said that?" She didn't know whether to be delighted or outraged. "You've discussed this, have you?"

"I got to Chelan last night," Seb said. "I couldn't get a boat and come up the lake until this morning. We had a lot of time to talk."

Neely opened her mouth and closed it again. "I don't know what to say," she murmured.

A corner of Seb's mouth lifted. "How about yes?"

"What would I be saying yes to, exactly?" She held her breath, daring to hope, but wondering if she was actually dreaming. Perhaps she'd been in the woods alone far too long.

"Yes to taking a chance on me for starters," Sebastian said. He dropped down on one knee next to the chair where she sat and took her hands in his. "Yes to letting me contribute a little light and space to those hotel plans you're working on—"

She caught her breath and blinked in surprise.

"—but mostly yes that you'll marry me because you are the woman I love, the one who gives light to my life and joy to my heart and—" he swallowed and went on, his voice ragged "—because wherever you are is home."

She leaned toward him, his arms came around her and as their lips touched she answered him. "Yes and yes and yes."

When Philip came later that afternoon, Seb told him to go away.

"Don't be rude," Neely protested.

Seb shrugged. "It shouldn't be any hardship. He goes away all the time."

Father's and son's eyes met in challenge, acknowledgment and acceptance. Philip nodded. "I'll see you tomorrow," he said to them. "It's a workday."

"We'll be there," Neely promised, even as Sebastian scooped her up in his arms and carried her back to bed.

They'd already been there once. And now once again they shared their bodies as well as their hopes and their dreams and their hearts. Only after, when they were lying wrapped in each other's arms, did Sebastian sit up and say, "I brought you something."

"What's that?"

"Well, a few things, actually," he confessed. "I'll be right back."

He yanked on his jeans and disappeared out the door. Bemused and baffled, Neely waited while he went down to the boat—twice—and then came back.

"This is for you," he said, holding out a package that had a shape she recognized at once.

With reverent hands, Neely took it and unwrapped it. "Your grandfather's violin?"

Seb nodded. "Yours now." And she knew the depth of his love from the gift of the one thing of enduring love he'd carried with him all his life.

"Play for me?"

"Here? Now? Naked on the bed?"

He nodded. "Please."

And so she sat up straight and tuned the strings and, after a moment, she began to play. She played a minuet. She played an étude. She played a favorite from her commune childhood, the simple folk hymn, "Morning Has Broken," because in fact, it had.

And when she was done, she handed him the violin and he set it on the dresser, then came down on the bed beside her and loved her again, with a tenderness and a warmth that showed her once again that Sebastian Savas wasn't an iceman at all.

And after she kissed him, then asked, "What else did you bring? You said you had two things."

He smiled. "Fish."

She sat up. "What? For dinner?"

He folded his arms behind his head, grinning now. "No. For the menagerie. They're what got me here. You gave my sisters the cats."

"Well, yes. But I didn't think you'd want them."

"And my stepmother the guinea pig," he went on. "And I was alone. And I remembered about the fish. You started with fish. So I did, too. But I don't have a clue about fish. So I thought you might be able to help me raise them."

Neely laughed. "I might be able to do that."

"And kids?" Sebastian said.

"As many as you want," she promised, her heart full to overflowing.

He rolled her beneath him and began to love her again. "What'd you do with the rabbits?"

She grinned. "I gave them to Max and Lara."